The Smug Pug

Anna Wilson

Illustrated by Clare Elsom

MACMILLAN CHILDREN'S BOOKS

First published 2013 by Macmillan Children's Books
a division of Macmillan Publishers Limited
20 New Wharf Road, London N1 9RR
Basingstoke and Oxford
Associated companies throughout the world
www.panmacmillan.com

ISBN 978-1-4472-0075-8

1 3 5 7 9 8 6 4 2

A CIP catalogue record for this book is available from
the British Library.

Printed and bound by CPI Group (UK) Ltd, Croydon CR0 4YY

For Millie Rule,
who wrote such a lovely story
for the PDSA Writing Competition

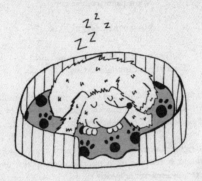

Hello Again and How Are You?

My, my, it seems an age since we last met. And if we haven't met before: hello and welcome to you, new reader!

As I am feeling particularly friendly today, I will give you a little introduction to the characters in Crumbly-under-Edge. (And if you are a reader who has already visited the town, I am sure you will be patient with me.)

This is Pippa Peppercorn, who is every bit as splendid as you. She is ten and three-quarters and a little bit more by now –

In other words, almost ELEVEN!

Quite! And she is the assistant in the pooch-pampering parlour and hair salon called Chop 'n' Chat.

The lady who owns the delightful salon is Mrs Semolina Ribena Fudge. (Although you must only ever call her Mrs Fudge, as she is not very fond of her first names.) Not only does she cut hair and pamper pooches most professionally, she is also a fabulous baker of cakes, meringues and biscuits.

Why, thank you, dear!

You are most welcome.

And this is Dash, the handsomest dachshund that ever there was.

Couldn't have put it better myself.

Yes, that's why I'm the author (ahem).

And this
is Muffles.

Miaaaoow!

She says she's delighted to meet you. And last, but
by no means least, here is Raphael, the friendliest
postman you are ever likely to meet.

Oh, darlin'!
I is blushin' now!

So now you
have met the main
characters (or said
hello to them all
again), let's get on
with the story!

1

Back to School (Groan)

Pippa Peppercorn woke to the sound of her alarm clock and immediately felt her heart sink to the bottom of her huge woolly bedsocks.

The alarm clock meant only one thing: school. It was the end of the Easter holidays, the end of lazy mornings. Lessons would begin that day and there was no getting out of it.

'I wonder if I could make up an excuse. I could say I have come down with some incredibly rare disease that makes it impossible for me to go to school ever again,' she pondered. She surveyed her clothes, which she had laid out the night before, and tried not to look at her book bag. 'Or I could pretend to be my mother calling by putting on a fake voice and saying, "I'm terribly sorry, but Pippa Peppercorn has been struck by lightning and will never be able to leave the house for the rest of her life." No, that wouldn't work. I wouldn't be able to go out to see Dash and Mrs Fudge then.' She sighed. 'It's ridiculous. I don't *need* to go to school. I can learn everything I will ever find necessary in life by going to Mrs Fudge's salon.'

And in some ways that was true. At Chop 'n' Chat, Pippa had to be good at many things. She had to be good at maths, so that she did not make mistakes with the money side of things (she never had yet). She also had to be good at English, so that she could deal with the letters-and-bills side of things (she always did that correctly). But, more importantly, she had to be good at speaking up and giving clear explanations so that she could handle the people side of things (she still had a *little* bit to learn in that department).

'And as these things are the skills you need in the big wide world,' Pippa went on, 'why on earth do I need to go to school to learn all the other stupid things they teach me? Like f'rinstance where America is. I don't need to know that, cos if I wanted to go I could just hop on a plane. It's not like I'd have to *row* there in a *boat* or anything.'

But she was a sensible girl and she knew there was no point in putting it off a moment longer. With a deep breath she threw herself at the pile of clothes and got dressed, grabbed her bag and slid down the banisters.

'I may as well make *something* fun about getting ready for school,' she said aloud.

Her boring parents were already at the kitchen table, noses firmly stuck in their newspapers and books, so Pippa snatched up a piece of toast, smeared it with peanut butter and ran out of the house yelling, 'It's the first day of term today. See you!'

(She had to remind her boring parents that it was the first day of term as they were so wrapped up in being boring that they would not have known where she was going otherwise.)

Pippa fetched her skateboard from the porch. She loved her skateboard as it meant she could travel speedily from A to B (or A to Z if it was a particularly long journey). It also gave her the rather pleasing sensation of the wind whistling in her ears as her red plaits flowed out behind her like bunting.

Now you might well ask, why would she want to get to school quickly if she didn't like school? And that would be a very sharp question, so full marks to you. But the reason Pippa loved her skateboard was that it was very useful for getting *away* from school in double-quick time. (And most days this was because she was going to help Mrs Fudge at Chop 'n' Chat.)

After a bit of whizzing along, Pippa realized she needed to slow down or she would arrive at school too early and have to spend time in the playground with other children. So she made a little detour to see one of Mrs Fudge's most loyal customers, Mrs

Prim, and offered to walk her springer spaniel, George. George always loved this as he got to run behind the speedy skateboard so that he too had the rather pleasing sensation of the wind whistling in his ears. And they looked even more like bunting fluttering in the breeze than Pippa's hair did!

Sadly the walk was over all too quickly and Pippa saw by her watch that she would have to rush otherwise she would be late.

'Which is as bad as being too early,' she explained to Mrs Prim, 'as everyone stares at you if you walk in late.'

So, once she had dropped George back, she pushed off schoolwards at full speed.

She arrived at St Crumble's Junior School, out of breath and with her hair all fluffed by the wind, just as the smallest boy was giving the school bell its final DONG, and as the last child was disappearing in through the door.

The head teacher was counting everyone in, and

9

when she saw Pippa she frowned and said, 'Pippa Peppercorn. How nice of you to join us.'

'Thank you,' said Pippa, thinking that it might be nice for the head teacher but it certainly wasn't at all nice for her. Then she slipped away to the cloakroom, where she stowed her skateboard under the benches, and sprinted to her classroom.

She was relieved to see that, rather than everyone being seated at their desks and staring at her for being late, the class was gathered around in a huddle, and from the middle of the huddle came a very loud voice that Pippa did not recognize.

'. . . and my parents have had to fly to Outer Zongolia to investigate the appearance of an extremely rare species of sky-blue-green bottle-nosed aphid,' said the very loud voice. 'So my grandfather, who is a professor and has just moved to Crumbly-under-Edge, has said I can stay with him.'

Oh *great*, a new girl, thought Pippa.

Pippa did not have a very good opinion of new

girls, as any new girl who had arrived in the past had immediately latched on to the Popular People and within minutes had been herded into a group with the whisperers and the sniggerers.

But as Pippa approached the circle of children, she caught a glimpse of the newcomer and immediately decided that *this* girl was decidedly different from any other she had ever seen.

For a start, she had MAD hair! Oh *boy*, did she have mad hair! It was wild and woolly and full of bounce and not a bit like the neatly brushed ponytails and topknots that the other girls had. And this hair was exactly the same shade of firework red as Pippa's. And the girl was wearing a pair of ginormous black-rimmed spectacles, which made her bright green eyes luminous and large. She wore a pencil behind each ear and her white dress looked a bit like a long white shirt which was too big for her. It was covered in pockets, which appeared to contain, among other things, more spectacles, more pencils, a ruler and a couple of

notebooks. Best of all, the funny new girl was ever
so slightly mischievous-looking. AND she had
something very interesting indeed peeking out of
her school bag, which no one else seemed to have
noticed yet.

'Is that a . . . ?' asked Pippa.

But she did not have time to finish her question,

as just then the form teacher, Mr Guttersnipe, came in and shouted at everyone to sit down.

But not before the girl had had a chance to grin broadly at Pippa and give her an enormous wink.

Introducing Tallulah Foghorn

There was an immediate and very crazy scramble as every child raced to sit in the seat they particularly wanted to sit in. And of course, everyone was clamouring to sit next to the new girl. New pupils were always exciting and they did not come along that often.

'Come and sit with me,' cooed Candida Smiley, the Most Popular Girl in the School. She patted the chair next to her, where her friend India Marmite usually sat. (India was for some reason sprawled on the floor beside her chair, rubbing her head and glaring angrily at Candida.)

But the new girl replied, 'No, thanks. I don't want to end up on the floor,' and, grabbing her bag, she plonked herself down next to Pippa (where there was always a free place).

'Hi!' she whispered hoarsely, ignoring Mr Guttersnipe, who was shooting her particularly dark looks.

Mr Guttersnipe then turned his back on the class and began writing on the board, so the new girl took Pippa's hand and pumped it up and down. 'I'm Tallulah. Tallulah Foghorn. What's your name?' she said. 'Oh, and this is Smug – but don't tell anyone he's here, will you?' She gestured to her school bag, where the small face of a particularly gorgeous-looking pug was concealed between a pencil case and yet another notebook. The little dog winked at Pippa.

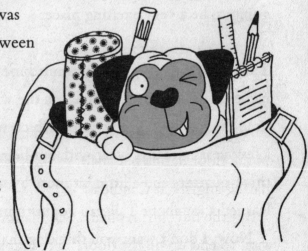

Well, that did it. Pippa's serious expression broke into the broadest of broad grins, her turquoise eyes went all glittery and she got one of those tingly feelings that you get in your tummy when you just know that you are going to be very good friends with someone. (You know the feeling. It makes you feel light and floaty and giggly and a tiny bit crazy, doesn't it?)

'I'm Pippa Peppercorn,' she whispered back, 'and it's very nice to meet you. Both of you!' she added, winking back at the pug.

For the first time in her life, Pippa felt school was going to be a very exciting place.

That day Pippa laughed and smiled more than she had ever done at St Crumble's in the whole long time she had been going there, which was quite a few years already, what with her being ten and three-quarters and a little bit more by now. And she learned a lot about Tallulah Foghorn in the process.

Now, I don't want you thinking that Pippa was

one of those naughty sorts of pupils who chatters and giggles in class whenever they think they can get away with it.

On the other hand, there is no point in trying to hide it: Tallulah *was* that sort of pupil. But because she was so incredibly brainy, she got away with it. For example, she was in the middle of telling Pippa that she liked to invent things. 'And Smug here is very useful at helping with all sorts of projects. In fact that is why I have brought him in today.' She explained that science was 'in my blood', as her parents were scientists of the travelling sort, who liked to 'swim rivers and climb mountains and wade through swamps to find interesting specimens to put in bottles and jars, so they never stay in the same place for more than a week—'

'Erm! Excuse me, Miss Foghorn!' Mr Guttersnipe butted in.

'Yes?' said Tallulah cheekily. 'What can I do for you?'

The whole class gasped in shock. And Candida

17

Smiley gave a particularly nasty snigger too, as she could see Tallulah was going to get into trouble.

Mr Guttersnipe raised his thick, hairy eyebrows and flared his thick, hairy nostrils and said, 'What you can do for me, Tallulah Foghorn, is to stop talking while *I* am talking!'

'Ah, technically you were *not* in fact talking at that moment,' Tallulah said, holding up a finger in a correcting sort of way. 'You were actually writing on the board, to be precise.'

'Tallulah,' said Mr Guttersnipe sharply, 'I'm afraid to tell you that I do not allow answering back in this class. Would you be so good as to tell me the answer to the question I just asked?' he added, glaring at the new girl.

'How can I answer the question if I am not allowed to answer back?' Tallulah pointed out.

There was another sharp intake of breath from the other pupils as Mr Guttersnipe's face went through several shades of purple before he shouted, 'Tell me the answer!'

Pippa glanced at her new friend and grimaced. She realized there was no way that Tallulah would be able to answer the question because she had not been listening.

Imagine her surprise when Tallulah replied: 'Well, why didn't you say that's what you wanted me to do? The answer is one hundred and fifty thousand, two hundred and sixty-two.'

How utterly amazing, thought Pippa. But she did not dare say so aloud, because Mr Guttersnipe was staring at Tallulah, who of course was right next to Pippa.

Mr Guttersnipe was in fact staring in an almost rude manner. His face had gone from purple to white, his jaw had dropped open and his spectacles had slipped off the end of his hairy nose and now fell to the floor with a clatter. He opened and closed his mouth a couple of times without one single squeak of a sound coming out.

Oh no, she's done it now, thought Pippa. He's

going to explode.
He's just building
up to it . . .

However, the
teacher merely
said, 'W-w-well,
I – I – yes, that's
very good,' in
a dazed tone of
voice. Then, clearing
his throat and
bending
down to
pick up
his spectacles, he

attempted to regain control of the situation. 'I am
glad to see that *someone* is paying attention,' he said
pointedly. He put his spectacles back on and looked
over the top of them at Pippa, who pretended to
find the ink stains on her desk very interesting
indeed.

'How did you do that?' she asked her new friend at break-time.

'What?'

'That thing where you were talking to me in the lesson but you were also listening to Mr Guttersnipe at the same time? At least I *suppose* you were listening at the same time, because otherwise how would you have known the answer?' Pippa babbled.

'Oh, it's all a case of extra-compensatory perception,' Tallulah said vaguely.

The pug in her bag let out a small snort.

Pippa chewed her lip and watched the pug carefully, but the little dog curled up and seemed to go to straight to sleep. Meanwhile Tallulah had cheerfully launched into another long story involving her parents and a rare species of parrot they had discovered, that could play the accordion and count backwards in Mandarin Chinese.

'This girl is fantastic,' Pippa said to herself. 'I do hope Dash likes her dog. Then we can have lots of fun together! I must find a way of introducing them.'

3

Dash Is Not Convinced

'MRS F., MRS F.!' cried Pippa, flinging open the door of Chop 'n' Chat. She propped her skateboard up against the wall, hurled her coat and scarf on to the pegs and skittered down the hall with a hop and a jump. 'You'll never guess what happened to me today!' she shouted.

She was so excited she couldn't wait until she was in the same room as Mrs Fudge before starting to speak. Although, had she stopped to think, she would have realized that it was a waste of effort, for Mrs Fudge (as you may remember if you have met her before) was a trifle deaf.

And even if Mrs Fudge had been able to hear perfectly through two brick walls and a closed door, the jolly old lady had her hands full as usual.

She was in the middle of dealing with a frisky Border terrier called Jasper whose whiskery face had become more than a little overgrown, which is not a good look for anyone. The whiskers had started to collect unwanted bits and pieces in them such as worms and pencil shavings and biscuit crumbs and Sellotape. Jasper's owner, a bright-as-a-button and delightful child called Millie Rule, was struggling to keep the pooch still while Mrs Fudge gently removed the offending items and combed the matted fur. She spoke soothingly to the irritable little dog as she worked.

'There, there, Jasper,' she was saying. 'I know it hurts a bit, but you've got so many nasty tangles. Nearly done . . .'

Dash was sitting at her feet, yapping out instructions to the dog and sounding a lot less gentle and understanding than Mrs Fudge was. 'Sit still, can't you? Mrs Fudge won't be able to do anything with you if you insist on twisting and turning like that.'

'Grrrrr,' said Jasper.

'There, there,' said Millie, copying Mrs Fudge's soothing manner.

'Miaaooow!' complained Muffles. The poor cat was trying to have forty winks on the countertop and was finding all these interruptions most aggravating.

'Ah, thank goodness you're here, Pippa,' said Mrs

Fudge, looking up. 'Could you give us a hand?' Mrs Fudge nodded to Dash, making it plain that she would find her job a lot easier without the noisy little dachshund under her feet. 'And perhaps a glass of lemonade for young Millie here,' she added, gesturing to the girl.

Mrs Fudge checked her late husband's gold pocket watch and tutted. 'Millicent Beadle will be here in five minutes.'

'Don't you want to hear about my new friends?' asked Pippa, as she scooped up a protesting Dash. But Mrs Fudge was wrestling with the terrier now and could only be heard to mutter, 'My, aren't we feisty? Why don't you take a seat, Millie dear, while Pippa brings some refreshments?'

'Yes, Mrs Fudge,' said Millie. She looked longingly at Pippa to emphasize how much she was looking forward to that glass of lemonade.

Pippa sighed and, taking the hint, made her way out to the kitchen. Dash struggled vigorously in her arms.

 26

'Do you mind?' he said irritably. 'I was helping Mrs Fudge. I do object to being picked up and thrown around the place without so much as a by-your-leave.'

'Actually,' said Pippa, once they were out of the salon so that Millie wouldn't hear her having a conversation with a dog, 'you were *not* helping. You were in the way. Now, why don't you stop yapping and listen to me?'

'Yapping?' protested Dash. 'YAPPING? I'll have you know—'

'Yes, I'm sure you will,' said Pippa. She put him down on the kitchen floor and stood over him, her hands on her hips.

Dash never liked it when she did this, as it only served to remind him how under-tall he was. He sat up on his stocky little haunches and held his head as high as he could, with his pointy nose in the air. It was his most distinguished look, and he knew how to use it for maximum effect.

'That's better,' said Pippa. She smiled wryly at

27

the proud miniature dachshund. She put the kettle on and then sat on a kitchen chair so that she was closer to Dash. 'What would you say if I told you that I have made a friend – at school?'

Dash flattened his ears and showed the whites of his eyes. 'Well,' he said, 'I'd say that was a turn-up for the books! I thought you hated the place and everyone in it.'

'I know. I do. I mean, I *have* done . . .' said Pippa, 'in the past. But everything's different now. There's this new girl and she is AMAZING. She doesn't care what anyone thinks about her, she took no notice of the Popular People like Candida Smiley and she has the most wonderful red hair just like me – only it isn't exactly like mine as it's big and whoofy and full of bounce, but it *is* red! And even better than all of this: she has a dog! I can't wait for you to meet them. I might bring them around tomorrow. Do you think Mrs F. would mind?'

'That depends . . .' Dash began.

But Pippa was not really interested in his opinion.

 28

She was too busy jabbering on about her new friend.

'She is *incredibly* clever and knows everything about everything! And her dog is a pug, like Coral Jones's dog Winston. And he is *gorgeous*. Tallulah brings him to school – that proves she is not like anyone else in that boring old place. None of the others would dare do that. He's so cute! And she lives with her grandfather who is a famous professor and her parents are famous scientists who travel all over the world –' she was getting a little carried away here, as Tallulah had said nothing whatsoever about her parents or grandfather being famous – 'and I'm sure you'll be the best of friends. We could go on walks, all four of us. Oh, I think life is going to be *perfect* from now on!' Pippa clasped her hands together and sighed happily.

Dash snarled softly. 'Just because you happen to think this girl's dog is "gorgeous", it does not necessarily mean that he and I will get along,' he said. 'Everyone in Crumbly-under-Edge has "gorgeous" dogs. That's why Mrs Fudge opened the pooch-pampering parlour, for heaven's sake. But I am not "the best of friends" with all of *them*, am I?'

Dash was clearly a little jealous. 'Do I need to remind you that you already have a friend? And a dog, for that matter?' he added huffily.

'What is the matter?' Pippa frowned, backing away slightly, for Dash's snarling had gone up a notch.

'*I* am your friend,' said the miniature dachshund. He spoke slowly and clearly as if speaking to someone of very little brain, 'and I am a dog.'

Pippa blushed. 'I know you are my friend, but you are not *my* dog, are you? You are not actually anyone's dog. You turned up in the middle of that storm and you wouldn't say where you'd come from. You live at Mrs Fudge's place, but I don't think even she would say that she owns you. You are *special* like that,' she added, warming to her theme. (She knew how to win Dash round, and it was working.)

'Yes, w-well – all right, I see what you mean,' said Dash. He looked up at Pippa bashfully, his chocolate-drop eyes wide and his feathery ears flat. 'I am very much my own dog, you are quite right. So, this newcomer. Tell me more.'

Pippa gave him a knowing smile. She could see that he was actually quite inquisitive, though he did not like to admit it. Then she told Dash everything she knew about Tallulah and Smug. As she spoke, she became more and more animated, and Dash, try as he might, found himself becoming more and more prickly. When Pippa told him the dog's name, he couldn't help yelping in amusement.

'*Smug?*' he squeaked. 'I bet he lives up to his name too.'

Pippa scrunched up her face into a particularly fearsome scowl and crossed her arms tightly across her chest. 'Well,' she said, 'if you're going to be like that, you won't be wanting to meet them, will you?'

'Meet who, dear?' asked Mrs Fudge. 'Have you got that glass of lemonade?'

A very thirsty Millie was right behind the old lady, and an equally thirsty Jasper was straining at his leash.

'See?' Dash muttered. 'You have already forgotten your responsibilities to your old friends.'

Pippa ignored him and beamed at Mrs Fudge. 'I was talking about my new friends!' she said. Then, seeing Millie's puzzled face, she said, 'I mean, I was *thinking* about my new friends. You can meet them yourself, Mrs Fudge. I will bring them to Chop 'n' Chat just as soon as I can.'

Then she whirled around before Dash could chip in with any more spiteful remarks and busied herself with fetching the refreshments.

4

Introduction Number Two: Smug the Pug

Pippa did not stop to eat her breakfast properly the next day, so anxious was she to get to school early. She flicked a piece of toast out of the toaster and whacked a dollop of apricot jam on it, then sped away on her skateboard before her parents had time to look up from their newspapers and notice she had gone.

Eating the toast and jam while skateboarding was a little bit of a palaver, as the morning was rather windy: Pippa's long red plaits kept being whisked into her mouth along with fragments of sticky toast. But even this inconvenience could not dampen our Pippa's spirits this morning as she sang with her mouth full of hair and breakfast.

'I'm off to see Tallulah!' she trilled. (To be honest, it was a good job her mouth *was* full of hair and toast, as Pippa had never been renowned for her singing voice, and this way no one could really hear her.)

She arrived in the playground to find Tallulah was already there, and she had brought Smug the pug with her again. He wasn't in Tallulah's bag this time though; he was sitting neatly by the new girl's enormous feet, which went some way to hiding him from general view. He was quietly watching as Tallulah smiled and waved at the other pupils who only the day before had been crowding around her, eager to get to know her. This time, though, they were walking straight past her and pretending that she didn't exist.

Oh dear, thought Pippa. Poor Tallulah.

For Pippa could see what the new girl clearly could not, which was that everyone had already decided *not* to be her friend. Tallulah was 'different', you see; for a start she had already proved that she was far too clever for their liking, and for a finish she did not 'fit in', whether it was because of her rather strange dress sense or her thick glasses or her crazy hair.

All of which were, of course, precisely why Pippa liked her.

However, even Pippa could see that some things about Tallulah might cause problems, and bringing Smug into school was one of them.

Surely she does not think she can bring her dog to school *every* day without one of the teachers noticing, Pippa thought. She must have a very odd idea of what school is like. Oh well. She shrugged and waved and called out to her new friend.

'Hi, Tallulah!' Pippa zoomed over and stopped in front of the girl and her dog, flicking her skateboard up with one black-booted foot and holding on to the top of it to stop it rolling away.

'Hello, Pippa,' said Tallulah. 'What a curious method of transporting yourself to school!' Then, picking up one of Pippa's plaits she peered at it short-sightedly and said, 'You also have an interesting line in hair accessories. Apricot jam! Most intriguing. I would never have thought of wearing it in such a manner. But it does look rather fetching on you, as it happens.'

Pippa stammered, 'Oh, er, yes. Thanks.' She took her plait back from her friend and began wiping at it. This girl is more than a little bit bonkers if she thinks I am actually wearing apricot jam on purpose! Pippa thought.

Tallulah was still speaking. 'I must say, I am relieved that you have made your presence known to me. I was beginning to think that we had accidentally switched on our latest invisibility invention before leaving the house this morning,' she said.

'I – er – what?' said Pippa.

'It seems that we cannot be seen by our fellow pupils this morning,' Tallulah explained.

Then Pippa realized what was going on.

'No! You are *not* invisible,' Pippa said firmly. 'The others were just being horrid and ignoring you. They do it all the time when they don't want to be friends with someone. Don't pay them any attention. *I* can see you very clearly,' she said. 'And, by the way, I can see Smug too – listen, I thought you said that you didn't want anyone to know about him? You should hide him away in your bag or you'll get into trouble.'

'Does she have to do that? It is awfully stuffy in there.'

Pippa started. 'Who said that?' She looked around, but the other children were continuing to walk past silently. 'Tallulah, did you just speak without moving your lips?' she asked.

'No, of course she didn't. She may be intelligent, but ventriloquism is most definitely not one of her skills.'

'Eh?' said Pippa, feeling more than a little bamboozled.

Tallulah merely giggled in response.

Pippa looked around her again, this time to see if anyone else had spoken and was perhaps playing a trick on her. But no one was so much as looking in her direction, let alone talking to her. Not even Candida Smiley (who was at that moment explaining that everyone had to play *her* latest skipping game to exactly and precisely *her* rules).

'I – I don't understand,' Pippa spluttered. 'If you didn't speak just then, Tallulah, who did?'

Tallulah clapped her hands, her green eyes twinkling. 'My, my! I had you marked out as special from the moment I met you, but I did not expect you to be quite so wonderful as all that.' She paused and looked at Pippa fondly, her head on one side.

'That's . . . that's really nice,' said Pippa. 'But could you explain what's going on, please?'

She felt a soft, wet nose prod at her calf and heard the mystery voice again: 'It certainly is wonderful to find a human who appreciates the finer species on this planet.'

Pippa looked down and saw that Tallulah's pug was looking back up at her and grinning.

Pippa gasped. And then she laughed. 'But . . . but this is FANTASTIC!' she cried.

'I agree,' said Tallulah. 'I had an inkling that you might be one of us, and now I am utterly convinced.'

'One of us – I – one of you?' Pippa said. 'What does that mean?'

But the bell rang for the beginning of lessons,

39

and the head teacher appeared in the doorway and shouted to everyone to line up to go inside.

This is so exciting! she thought. Dash is going to LOVE these two.

5

Mrs Fudge Gets Rather Cross

That afternoon when Pippa went to Chop 'n' Chat she talked of nothing but Tallulah and Smug. A very bored Dash soon took himself into the kitchen, curled up in his basket and went to sleep.

Sadly Mrs Fudge was soon fed up with Pippa's constant chatter too. Especially when it became clear that Pippa was so fizz-poppingly excited that she was not paying full attention to the customers.

'Pippa, dear,' said Mrs Fudge, struggling to keep her voice kindly and calm, 'I feel you are a little distracted this afternoon.'

But Pippa was still chattering away. 'And then Tallulah said—'

'PIPPA!' cried Mrs Fudge.

'Oh, sorry, what?' said Pippa.

'As I was saying – I feel you are a little *distracted*.' Mrs Fudge nodded towards the dog-grooming table, where Penelope Smythe was perched, looking quite anxious (as well she might, seeing as Pippa was pointing some dog clippers in her direction). Then the old lady gestured to a twirly-whirly chair where Penelope's saluki, Sukie, was sitting contentedly, a cape and a towel around her neck, her tongue lolling happily out of the corner of her mouth.

'OH!' cried Pippa, rushing to correct the situation. She charged

at Penelope, with the intention of helping her down from the table, but she was still holding the clippers. The poor lady needed no more proof that she was about to be groomed instead of her pooch. She screamed loudly and leaped in the air. She landed with a thud on Muffles, who had chosen that moment to stalk a spider that had scuttled in from the garden.

'Help!' cried Penelope.

'Raaaooow!' shrieked Muffles. (The spider said nothing, but made a clean getaway.)

'Woof-woof-woof!' exclaimed Sukie, who immediately assumed a game had started and bounded off the twirly-whirly chair to chase Muffles out of the salon.

Mrs Fudge was sent spinning as the dog knocked her off balance.

'That does it!' she shouted above the cacophony. 'I'm going to have to ask you to go home, Pippa.'

'I should say so!' agreed Penelope crossly, picking herself up.

'But – I'm – I'm so sorry,' spluttered Pippa.

'It's no good you being here, dear,' said Mrs Fudge, 'if your mind is elsewhere. You can come back when you are ready to be useful again. I would rather have my hands full than have you cause such a commotion.'

Poor Pippa. She never meant to cause anyone any trouble, let alone her dear friend Mrs Fudge. And she had never heard the lovely old lady sound so cross with her before. But as she surveyed the scene that she had helped to bring about, she realized that she must do as she was told. 'All right,' she said quietly. 'I'll go.'

The next day Tallulah and Smug were late, so Pippa did not get a chance to talk to them until break-time. So she fidgeted and wriggled during lessons, itching for the bell to hurry up and ring so that she could run outside into the playground and talk to her new friends.

But then, who would *not* fidget and wriggle if they had a person such as Mr Guttersnipe for their teacher? The minute he arrived in the classroom he was shouting out such teacherly nonsense as, 'Sit down and shut up and use your ears and mouth in their correct proportions.' And then he warbled on, explaining a maths problem which would demonstrate how many apples it takes to make Susie decide to swim across the Channel with only one flipper (or something).

Mr Guttersnipe could have announced that he was giving away free chocolate and Pippa would not have reacted because she just could not concentrate on what he was saying.

45

I *have* to find a way to get Tallulah and Smug to Chop 'n' Chat, she was thinking. I know Mrs Fudge and Dash will love them once they have met them. But Mrs Fudge was so cross with me yesterday. Perhaps she will not ever want *me* back, let alone want to meet my friends? she thought sadly. Unless I can do something extra-specially nice for her that will make her pleased with me again.

'Pippa Peppercorn!' An annoying nasal voice broke into her sad thoughts.

Pippa looked up and saw an enormous pair of hairy nostrils. It was like staring into a snotty forest.

'Urgh!' she said.

'No, Miss Peppercorn,' said Mr Guttersnipe (for that is who the nostrils belonged to). 'That is not the answer I was looking for.'

The whole class sniggered.

Pippa felt a tap on her knee and looked down to see Smug holding out a piece of paper to her.

'Read it out,' the pug hissed.

Pippa looked up nervously. Mr Guttersnipe's nostril hairs were still dangerously close and the class's sniggering was becoming louder.

'So, as I thought,' sneered the teacher, 'you were not paying attention. In which case, I suggest that you stay behind after school and—'

'Fifty-six metres per second,' Pippa said loudly.

'Report to the Head at—' Mr Guttersnipe began. Then, 'Oh, right . . . so you *were* listening. That's – that's

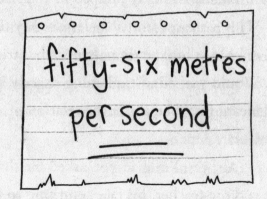

very good, Pippa,' he said. He straightened up and coughed to cover his embarrassment. 'Yes, well, in future it would be nice if you replied straight away, rather than making me come over and wring the answer out of you.'

And in future it would be nice if you didn't lean in so close and show me all your nostril hairs, thought Pippa.

At least she *thought* she had thought it, but the teacher's face went a deep shade of purple and he spluttered, 'WHAT did you just say, Pippa Peppercorn?'

Tallulah quickly jumped in and said loudly, 'This is a most *fascinating* lesson. My teachers at my old school never taught such intriguing things. Would you mind explaining exactly what you meant just then about the relation of x to y, Mr Guttersnipe?'

'Ah, yes, I'm glad you asked me that, Tallulah,' said the teacher, his face returning to its normal colour. 'It is always lovely to have intelligent questions from the class.'

(Teachers are so easy to distract in this manner. Try it sometime. You'll be amazed. You really will.)

 48

The rest of the class rolled their eyes and muttered 'geek' and 'weirdo' under their breath, but Pippa smiled gratefully at her new friend and reached down to give Smug a quick pat.

6

Pippa Gets an Invitation

Finally the bell rang and Pippa skedaddled out of the classroom to get ahead of everyone else.

'Tallulah,' she said breathlessly, beckoning her over to the furthest corner of the playground, 'I need to talk to you.'

'OK,' said Tallulah. 'What's up? You seem rather downcast.'

Pippa sniffed. 'I am a bit sad, yes. It's all cos of something that happened at Mrs Fudge's pooch-pampering parlour last night.'

'A pooch-ering what?' asked Tallulah, blinking.

'It's a hairdressing salon and a dog-grooming business all rolled into one. Only I managed to roll it quite literally into one yesterday by mixing up my customers and now Mrs Fudge is cross with me. And it's a nightmare, because she needs my help because she is always so busy, but after what happened yesterday I think maybe she doesn't want me back again.' Pippa paused to catch her breath.

Tallulah tutted. 'That does sound serious.'

'And I was so looking forward to introducing you to her. And to Dash.'

'Dash?' asked Smug, from inside Tallulah's bag.

'Yes. He's a dachshund. And he's just like you!' Pippa added, perking up a bit.

Smug coughed apologetically. 'I, er, I doubt that he is,' he said seriously. 'There is no one quite like me. And as for comparing me to a dachshund . . .'

Pippa smiled. 'What I mean is, I can understand him just like I can understand you. So can Mrs Fudge. I did think that the four of us would make a great team, but—'

'And so we shall,' said Tallulah. 'I have just had the most marvellous brainwave. You say Mrs Fudge is busy in this pampering place?'

'Very,' said Pippa.

'And you would like to get back into her good books?' Tallulah went on.

'Of course!' said Pippa.

'And you are worried that the old lady is overworked.'

'Yes, yes,' said Pippa impatiently.

'Are you thinking what I am thinking, Smug?' Tallulah said to her school bag.

'I – I rather hope not,' came a muffled reply.

'Excellent,' said the funny girl. 'In that case, Pippa, you are warmly invited to come around to my grandfather's house this afternoon where I can show you the Inventionary and unveil my grand plan.'

'Talking to yourself again, are you?'

Candida Smiley had appeared at Pippa's elbow with India Marmite in tow. Candida was smiling her nastiest smile and India was looking at her adoringly, as she always did.

'No, I am not talking to myself,' Pippa said. 'I am

talking to my friend Tallulah and . . .' She stopped herself before she said the words 'and her dog', as clearly that would not have been a sensible thing to say to a girl such as Candida.

'Oh? And what *friend* would that be?' asked Candida. She made her face look wide and innocent and glanced about her curiously. 'Only I can't see anyone here except me and India. And we,' she added, smiling that nasty smile again, 'are obviously not your friends.'

'Hey!' protested Tallulah. 'That is an extremely unpleasant thing to say. In any case—'

'What was that?' Candida interrupted. 'India, did you just hear a funny whining noise?' She made a big show of cupping her hand around her ear and listening intently.

'No,' said India. 'I did hear that stupid new girl, though – Ow!' Candida had pinched her.

'I think we had better leave Pippa Pathetic Peppercorn to her imaginary friend,' said Candida.

53

Tallulah stepped right in front of Candida and leaned forward so that her long nose was almost touching the tip of Pippa's tormentor's nose and said, 'Look. I am a real person. I am standing right here. What is your problem?'

Candida wrinkled her little button nose and said, 'Urgh. There is a particularly nasty smell around here. It stinks of clever-two-shoes-ness and I-think-I'm-so-great-ness.' She pulled an expression of deep disgust. 'I think we should go, India, before it makes me throw up.'

India frowned. 'I can't smell—'

But Candida grabbed her by the sleeve and dragged her off, sniggering and making loud comments about 'geeks with smelly weird hair'.

Pippa was so angry her plaits were practically shooting sparks out of the ends. 'The only smell around here is coming from YOU!' she shouted after the two nasty girls.

Tallulah laid a large hand on her arm. 'Don't you worry about them,' she said. 'They are clearly inferior intellectually.'

'Eh?' said Pippa.

'They're stupid,' said Smug with a sigh. 'And we are not. And seeing as Tally is intent on taking you home with us this afternoon, once you get there you will understand just how marvellous we actually are.'

7

The Incredible Inventionary

'Come to the bike shed when you are ready,' said Tallulah. 'I need to fetch our method of transportation.'

Pippa's eyes went as round as a couple of spacehoppers (although not as orange) when she saw what Tallulah was talking about. 'Is — is that *really* yours?' she stammered, pointing.

'Oh, this old jalopy?' said Tallulah casually. 'Yes, in a manner of speaking.'

Pippa gasped. The vehicle her friend had brought out of the back of the bike shed was not the sort of thing a child normally goes to school on. It was a brightly painted, bubble-gum-pink sort of scooter-mobile, the like of which Pippa had never seen before (and I'm sure you won't have done either). It looked as though it had been made out of old car and bicycle and aeroplane parts, all stuck together. And, to make it extra-special, it had a tiny pink sidecar attached.

And even more wonderfully extra-special was the sight of what was in the sidecar: for quick as a flash, Smug had found his way in and was now sitting upright, his little face scrunched inside a particularly fetching bright pink helmet! He was so adorably cute: his pudgy soft face with folds of fur looked even more wrinkly than usual because of the helmet, which seemed to scrunch up his jowls. You would have just wanted to scoop him up there and then and snuggle him tight, I can assure you.

Pippa hugged herself with excitement. If this scooter-mobile was even a hint of things to come at Tallulah's house, she could not wait to get there. 'Come on then!' she said. 'Let's not waste a second. Show me the way to your grandfather's.'

She hopped on to her skateboard and leaned forward, ready to push off. Tallulah put on her own pink helmet, climbed into the scooter-mobile and revved up the engine.

'I don't mean to be a spoilsport,' Smug shouted to Pippa above the racket, 'but will you be able to keep up with us?' Tallulah turned out of the school gate and took off down the road at speed.

Pippa set her jaw. 'Just you watch!' she cried, and she kicked off with a *zoom*! She caught up with the scooter-mobile in five seconds flat, a cloud of dust rising from the road behind her.

'My, my!' shouted Tallulah as Pippa drew level with her. 'Your exceptionally intriguing method of transport certainly results in your travelling at quite a velocity.'

'What are you on about?' cried Pippa.

'You go fast on that thing!' explained Smug.

'Yeeeehah!' Pippa punched the air with her fist and the friends tore through Crumbly-under-Edge, attracting some very hostile stares from the townsfolk as they went.

The professor's house was on the outskirts of the other side of town and was even bigger and more rambling than Mrs Fudge's place. Pippa did not take in many details, as she was so eager to get inside and see the Inventionary. Smug had run on ahead.

'I told him to put the kettle on,' said Tallulah.

'Really?' Pippa was puzzled. Surely he was not as clever as all that, she thought.

But it seemed he was even cleverer than she could have imagined. As the two girls walked down the long dark entrance hall, Smug reappeared from a back room. The little pug was carrying something in his mouth. Pippa saw that it was a small book, and that he also had a yellow pencil tucked behind one ear.

'Smug, what is that book?' Pippa asked. 'And why have you got a pencil tucked behind your ear?'

The pug dropped the notebook so that he could answer. 'Oh, I thought I might finish off a crossword while I waited for the kettle to boil. I do like a good crossword. This is my notebook where I do my workings-out and scribblings before I fill in the puzzles. Quite a fan of Sudoku too after my afternoon nap,' he said carelessly. 'Keeps the grey matter ticking over, don't you know?'

'I – don't know, no,' said Pippa.

'Such a brain!' Tallulah said affectionately. 'Have you seen Grandfather?' she added, nodding into the house.

'I am afraid he seems to have gone out somewhere,' said the pug vaguely. 'He left this note.' He flicked open the notebook with his paw to reveal a scrap of paper contained within its pages. 'Here you are,' he said, pushing the paper towards the girls.

Pippa peered over her friend's shoulder at the message on the paper. She frowned. It looked like gobbledygook to her.

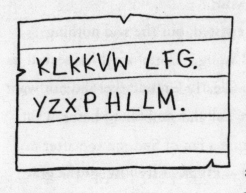

Tallulah read the note aloud. 'A bit scant on information,' she said. 'Ah well. Sorry about this, Pippa. You'll have to meet him another time.'

'But – but – what language is that?' Pippa asked.

Smug gave a little snort. 'It's not a *language*. It's a *code*,' he said.

Tallulah hushed him and said gently, 'It's a simple substitution cipher. It is quite easy to read once you know how: you merely take your original units of plain text and replace them with cipher text, according to a regular system—'

'Well, if it's so simple,' interrupted Pippa impatiently, 'then what is the point in using it?'

Smug put his head on one side. '*You* don't understand it, do you?'

Pippa's mouth twisted, but she said nothing.

'Precisely,' said Smug. 'Therefore it has served its purpose as a code. Clearly Grandfather did not want anyone other than Tallulah and me to know what he had written.'

Tallulah smiled at Pippa. 'I'll show you how it works. Look.' She pointed at the letters. 'For a start there are repeated letters, so that is an instant clue.'

'I don't get it,' Pippa sulked. 'Just tell me what it says.'

Smug raised his eyebrow again at Tallulah, who said, 'Grandfather's written, "POPPED OUT. BACK SOON" – as I say, not a very informative note. He has simply used the alphabet backwards to write his note. The K is P, the L, O and so on. Look, I'll show you.'

She took a pencil from behind her ear and turned over the note that her grandfather had written. Then she wrote out the whole alphabet from A to Z and then above it she wrote the whole alphabet from Z to A.

ZYXWVUTSRQPONMLKJIHGFEDCBA
ABCDEFGHIJKLMNOPQRSTUVWXYZ

Then she pointed at the letters as she explained how the code worked. 'If you want to write A in this code, you use Z instead. So that's why P becomes K and O becomes L.'

Pippa's face brightened as she understood. 'That is brilliant!' she cried. 'We can write notes to each other in class now and no one will understand them!'

Smug rolled his eyes. 'You're probably right,' he said. 'From what I have seen of your classmates (and your teacher, come to that), I doubt any of them would understand a substitution cipher either. Now, are you going to show Pippa the Inventionary at least?'

'Come and see,' said Tallulah, linking arms with Pippa.

'But no touching anything in there,' Smug warned. 'We are in the middle of a particularly tricky idea just at the minute.'

'What do you mean, "we"?' said Pippa.

'He means "he", as in my grandfather,' said

Tallulah hastily. '*Grandfather* is stuck on a project. Let's take a look!'

'Oh, come, come,' said Smug. 'I think we can tell her.' He shot Tallulah a cryptic glance.

'Tell me WHAT?' cried Pippa.

Tallulah shrugged. 'If you're sure.'

'Please tell me!' Pippa begged.

Tallulah smiled. 'All right. Smug helps Grandfather with his inventions. But you really mustn't tell *anyone*,' she insisted, 'because there is no other dog in the world as clever as he is, and people might want to dognap him if they knew about his skills.'

Pippa shook her head in astonishment and skipped through the house with Tallulah, Smug trotting along at their heels. What a pair! she thought. And what a house!

It was chock-full to the rafters with stuff so that you had to squeeze between things to get from one room to the next. In fact it looked to Pippa more like a car-boot sale than a house. Every available space on the walls was covered in paintings and framed photographs (most of them of Tallulah and Smug, a few of an elderly gentleman who, apart from the bushy beard and moustache, looked spookily like an older male version of Tallulah, with the same green eyes and thick, black-rimmed specs and masses of whoofy, bushy, crazy hair, which was red, just like his granddaughter's).

Every spare centimetre of floor space was covered in furniture, and, Pippa noticed as she peered into rooms off the hallway, every piece of furniture had piles and piles of paper on its surface. Even the ceilings seemed to have objects hanging from them, including some very odd-looking devices held together with ropes and string and attached to wheels and cogs and levers. It all looked rather terrifying to Pippa, who was very careful not to touch a single thing.

What on earth are these inventions for? she wondered.

At last, after passing through the kitchen to collect huge mugs of tea, they came to the end of the tour and Tallulah flung open a door which was covered in pinned-on scraps of paper, each piece full of unintelligible scribblings, numbers and diagrams.

'The Inventionary!' she announced proudly.

If the rest of the house had made Pippa feel dizzy, this room made her feel as though someone had taken her to the highest roller coaster in the world and pushed her down without strapping her in.

'Whoa!' she cried, bedazzled by the blinking lights and whirring sounds and flashing screens. 'What in the highest heavens—?'

'We are in the middle of creating a device that does all the housework at once,' announced Smug. 'I thought I would call it the Household Helper.'

'It's a sort of cleaner-ironer-washer-upper,' explained Tallulah, pointing to an ironing board which was sticking out of one side of the invention, and a dish rack on the other. 'And, as Smug has said, it is not quite ready yet.'

'We are still working on a few details,' added Smug. He padded over to the machine and put a plate in the dish rack.

'Smug, I don't think you should . . .' began Tallulah.

But the little dog had nudged a red button with his nose and the plate was suddenly catapulted into the air and landed on the ironing board. A lever came out of a small door, bringing with it an iron, which then dropped on to the plate and promptly smashed it.

'Ahem, as you can see, just an *infinitesimal* amount of fine-tuning is needed,' said Tallulah. She narrowed her eyes and held up her finger and thumb to emphasize that only the tiniest of changes were required.

Pippa giggled but then caught sight of Smug, who did *not* seem to find Tallulah's teasing funny. 'All right, all right,' he muttered. 'Won't be hard to fix.'

He stood on his hind legs and reached up to a small lever that Pippa had not noticed before. As he gave it a quick tap with one of his front paws, a drawer opened just beneath it. Two mechanical hands appeared holding a dustpan and brush and proceeded to sweep up the broken shards of crockery.

Pippa breathed in sharply.

'It is a relief to find the sweeping-up section is functioning at least,' said Smug.

'Which is what brings me to my idea,' said Tallulah.

'You have an idea on how to fix the Household Helper?' said Pippa.

'If it's to do with the sub-coordinator in the lower ratchets of the carbonator, your grandfather and I have already tried that,' said Smug sadly.

'No, no. I was thinking of another invention entirely,' said Tallulah. She wiggled her ears and her black-rimmed spectacles jumped up and down on her nose. 'You were saying that you wanted to get back into the good books of your Mrs Fudge?'

'Oh yes,' said Pippa. 'I would love to show her that I can still be useful to her.'

'Well, luckily for you, we can design JUST the machine to help.'

'Steady on, Tallulah. I don't know if the professor would be willing to let any of his machines out of the house,' said the pug sternly.

 70

'Oh, don't be a killjoy,' Tallulah said. 'Don't you see? This is the perfect opportunity to develop a machine and give it a thorough testing. It is a win-win situation.'

Smug washed one paw thoughtfully. 'Hmm. I suppose so,' he said.

'He can't resist a challenge!' cried Tallulah. 'Now, Smug, why don't you show Pippa some of your other inventions?'

The pug clearly could not resist showing off either. Pippa watched in amazement as he hopped lightly down from the table to give a demonstration of a smaller invention, which was designed to vacuum the floor without the need for a human to push it around. It was very impressive.

He then leaped daintily into an old bathtub which had a series of buttons on it. He pushed one and a shower cap was popped neatly on to his head. Another button was pressed and the bath taps turned themselves on, and after pressing yet another button, sweet-smelling bubble bath was poured into

the bath which then filled with warm water and
mounds of big shiny bubbles.

'Aaah, lovely!' said Smug, closing his eyes. Then
he leaped back out, flicked a switch and a pair of
white-gloved hands emerged from the side of the
bath. They removed the shower cap and produced a
towel. The towel was wrapped around Smug and he
was given a vigorous scrub.

'What do you think?' Smug asked, raising one eyebrow. 'It's one of my more recent projects.'

'It's – it's awesome,' said Pippa, in hushed tones.

Smug came back to sit with the girls. 'Right. Down to work. Can you pass me some paper and a pencil, please? Oh, and my specs. Thank you.'

The dog lifted his head for Tallulah to place an oversized pair of thick-framed spectacles identical to her own on his flat little face. He wrinkled his nose to settle them into place, then, taking a pencil between his claws, he began to draw shapes and arrows and lots of squiggly things. Soon the page was covered.

'What is he doing?' Pippa hissed.

'Shh,' said Tallulah. 'He's concentrating. Don't stop him in mid-flow.'

Smug muttered to himself and scribbled and scrawled and was soon writing on the table itself, since he had run out of space on the paper. Pippa wondered if she should say something, as he didn't seem to have noticed. Then she took in her surroundings again and realized that, in a house such as this, a scribbled-on table was quite probably the least of anyone's worries.

At last Smug cleared his throat noisily and said, 'Let's see now. If x equals y equals z and a quarter, then no one has any idea what they are talking about, *but* if I were to multiply the signs of the zodiac backwards while adding pi to the square root of a million and fifty-six, then – oh my goodness!' he exclaimed, twitching his nose (which made the thick-rimmed spectacles dance around his funny little face). 'Eureka!'

'You reek o' what?' cried Pippa. She jumped up from her chair in alarm and looked around wildly.

Smug shook off his spectacles with a snigger. 'I said, "Eureka!"'

'It's ancient Greek for "I have found it!"' Tallulah explained.

'Found *what*?' said Pippa.

Tallulah scrambled to her feet and peered at

Smug's notes and jottings. 'The solution to your problem.'

'Indeed,' said Smug. 'How would your Mrs Fudge react, do you think, if we told her that she could have a machine that can help her with haircutting so that she can concentrate on the dog grooming?'

'Brilliant!' exclaimed Pippa. 'That is exactly what she needs.'

'Good, good. Well, leave it with us. We should have it knocked together in, ah, um, what do you think, Tally?' The pug gestured to the sketches and notes.

'I should say we could have it ready by tomorrow. If we work flat out through the night, that is,' said Tallulah.

'R-really?' Pippa said, astounded. She looked at the scrawlings and suddenly felt overcome with doubt that such a complicated-looking invention could be built in such a short space of time.

'Indubitably,' said Tallulah.

'She means "of course",' Smug translated with a smirk.

Pippa clapped her hands and shouted, 'Hooray! If this doesn't get me back into Mrs Fudge's good books, I don't know what will.'

8

Dash and Smug Finally Meet

Pippa went straight around to Chop 'n' Chat after school the next day. She had travelled even faster than usual so that, by the time she arrived at the old house on Liquorice Drive, she felt as though every last breath had been squeezed out of her.

I must sound grown-up and clever about the whole thing, she told herself. Tallulah would not rush in and gabble away like an overexcited schoolgirl. And Smug would be extremely intelligent and logical.

She allowed herself one squeal of excitement and two claps of her hands before saying, 'Calm yourself, Pippa Peppercorn'. Then she let herself

77

into the house as quietly and normally as she could.

But she forgot all her own advice the minute she saw Dash coming to the door to greet her.

'Good afternoon, Pippa,' said the little dachshund. 'Nice of you to drop by. I wasn't sure if you had time for your *old* friends any more.'

If Pippa had not been in such a hurry to tell Dash about the invention, she might have pointed out that it was her old friends who had not had time for her. But instead she said in a rush, 'They said they would come along this afternoon – and they would bring it with them.' Her eyes were shining. 'I can't wait for Mrs Fudge to meet everyone. And for you to meet them too,' she added.

'And who is "they" and what is "it"?' asked Dash irritably. (He did of course know the answer to the first question.)

'THE FOGHORNS!' cried Pippa, bouncing up and down on the tips of her toes. 'TALLULAH AND SMUG THE PUG AND THE PROFESSOR

 78

AND THEIR MAGNIFICENT SURPRISE FOR
YOU!'

'Oh, *them*,' said Dash, sticking his pointy little
nose in the air. 'That reminds me – Raphael came
in earlier with the post. He said there are a lot
of strange goings-on and peculiar noises coming
from the Foghorns' house. I think you should be
careful—'

'Anyway, so they are coming round, and it's very
important we are all friendly and nice!' Pippa cut
in. 'And Tally thinks they have almost cracked their
design, and Smug says that it might still need a few
bits of "fine-tuning and last-minute adjustments",'
she babbled.

'Design? Machine?' asked Dash. His curiosity was
piqued now.

'Oh, did I not say? They have designed a machine
that is going to help out in Chop 'n' Chat when
there are too many customers. It might need a bit of
work still—'

'A machine? Which needs "a bit of work"? Load

79

of old rot,' muttered Dash. 'Sounds more like your *friends* are using code for "I've promised something I can't deliver" or "I've made a huge mistake and I'm going to have to start all over again".'

'Dash, will you stop being so rude?' Pippa snapped. 'You haven't even met them and you're already being horrible.'

'And all you've done since they arrived is go on and on about Tallulah – sorry, *Tally* this and *Smug* that and how *amazing* they are,' growled Dash.

'Oh, so that's it!' cried Pippa, flinging her hands in the air. 'You're jealous, aren't you? You can't bear it that I have other friends.'

Dash put his tail between his legs and scuttled off to his basket in the kitchen.

'Pippa!' said Mrs Fudge. She had overheard the end of the unpleasant exchange between her two friends and she was not happy. She looked at Pippa over the top of her half-moon spectacles. 'Lovely to see you. I hope you are going to be more of a help than a hindrance today, my dear.'

'Yes. Sorry, Mrs Fudge,' said Pippa, lowering her eyes. 'I promise that I won't let any disasters happen again. By the way,' she said, brightening, 'I have organized for my new friends to come round so that you can finally meet them.'

Mrs Fudge softened. 'That's a lovely idea. But perhaps not today. I'm run off my feet and—'

The doorbell cut her off and Dash went tearing down the hallway, barking, 'I'll get it!' (Poor Dash never remembered that even if he stood up on his hind legs he was not able to reach the door handle.)

Muffles had been skulking in the doorway, eavesdropping on all the hoo-ha. She leaped into the air, hissing angrily, as Dash rushed past.

''Scuse me, Muffles,' gasped Pippa, hot on Dash's tail. She pushed past the dachshund and got to the door before him.

'Hi!' said Tallulah, as Pippa flung open the front door. 'We would have brought Grandfather too, but he had a previous engagement. And he did so want to meet you all.'

Smug trotted in behind Tallulah, his nose in the air and an expression of extreme satisfaction on his soft, wrinkled face. He was wearing his thick-rimmed spectacles again.

Hmm, thought Dash. Looks like a bit of a geek. He made his tail stand as high as he could and pricked his ears up to show that he was the boss of the house.

But Smug either did not notice this body language, or did not care. He trotted right up to give the dachshund a friendly lick on the nose.

 82

'Friends?' he said. Then before Dash could disagree, he added briskly, 'Now, enough chit-chat. Where do you think the machine should go, Mrs Fudge?'

'Machine? I – Did he just . . . ?' Mrs Fudge's face had gone as white as her hair. She was pointing at Smug with one hand and fanning her face with the other.

'Yes, I did,' said Smug. 'And if you don't mind my saying, I don't see why you should be so surprised. After all, Dash can make himself understood by humans, so why shouldn't I?'

'Sorry, Mrs Fudge,' said Pippa. 'I should have said.'

'Great,' Dash mumbled. 'That's all I need.'

Mrs Fudge put on an extra-jolly voice to try to lighten the atmosphere. 'Well, it's wonderful to have yet another intelligent, charming pooch around the place.' She ruffled Dash's fur to make it clear he was not to be left out, then said, 'Shall we all come through to the kitchen?'

She produced a plate piled high with pink, green and violet macaroons and a pot of tea, and everyone tucked in while chattering noisily. Muffles crept in unnoticed under cover of the gossip and munching and settled herself in her favourite armchair, curling her tail protectively around herself.

Dash eyed the cat with envy and wished he could withdraw from the party going on around him. He found himself feeling more than a little suspicious of the pug. Smug had chosen to sit on a chair up at the table, which Dash found very un-doglike. He himself sat resolutely at Pippa's feet and listened carefully.

Who does he think he is? Dash thought as he observed Smug. And who ever heard of a dog wearing glasses? He shuddered. Next thing you know he'll be wearing a suit and tie and drinking tea from a cup!

There is something not right about this animal,

Dash decided. And I don't like the sound of this machine either. I think I am going to have to keep a close eye on these Foghorns. A very close eye indeed . . .

9

Who Will Try the New Machine?

At last tea was finished and Tallulah offered to set up the machine. 'Because Smug is all paws and claws when it comes to putting it together,' she explained.

But, as it turned out, she made quite a mess of it herself. She became more and more flustered as Smug shouted instructions at her, running every which way and yapping the whole time. Dash watched in horror as the dog leaped up on to the counter and jumped from there to the twirly-whirly chairs, clearing the surfaces in the salon as he went by, sweeping the bottles of shampoo and the brushes and curling tongs on to the floor.

Meanwhile Tallulah unplugged all the hairdryers

and placed a pile of beautifully folded towels on to the sofa. Then she rushed around like a whirlwind with armfuls of wires and plugs, fixing them into the sockets and muttering to herself as she went.

'Raaaoooooow!' Muffles was not amused as she had been having a particularly satisfying dream about chasing a mouse, and all this noise and kerfuffle had woken her up.

'Excuse me!' barked Dash. 'Could you please be more careful? It took us ages to—'

'Dash,' said Mrs Fudge, 'don't interrupt. I am sure Tallulah needs to concentrate.'

'Yes,' agreed the girl. 'It is very important to be focused while working. Tidying up can always wait. That is what Grandfather says.' She frowned as she peered at two more plugs in her hand and searched for more sockets. 'Aha!' she said, spotting one near a dog basket by the floor. She reached for the plug that was already there and pulled it out.

Dash growled. 'That was my electric blanket,' he complained. 'I was warming that up for later.'

Honestly, he thought again, who DO they think they are? Coming here with their long words and stupid inventions . . .

Tallulah meanwhile was twisting and turning all manner of dials and cogs and buttons. The machine started to click and hum and hundreds of tiny coloured lights began flashing on and off in a pretty pattern.

'Oooh!' said Mrs Fudge.

'Aaah!' said Pippa.

Tallulah was keeping up a running commentary on what she was doing, and as most of the words she used were impossibly long and confusing, Smug had to chip in with slightly easier-to-understand explanations along the way.

'She's saying that that button there will be the one to use for a quick trim,' he said, indicating a small red button which looked alarmingly similar to a number of other small red buttons. Pippa decided she would ask her friends to produce some sticky labels so that she and Mrs Fudge would not get confused when they came to use the machine.

'And this mechanical arm here,' Smug went on, 'will be useful for mixing hair dye, and this hand here can be used to apply the dye—'

'I'm beginning to wonder if this machine might take over from me completely,' said Mrs Fudge. She was trying to sound light and jokey, but there was a hint of wobbliness in her voice.

'Well, now you come to mention it,' began Smug, 'I think you'll find that the machine will free you up to—'

Dash could not keep quiet a moment longer. 'Now listen here!' he exploded. 'No one and nothing, not even the world's most fantastically designed *robot*, could replace Mrs Fudge! She is totally one hundred per cent irreplaceable. Isn't she, Pippa? Pippa . . . ?'

But once again, no one was listening to Dash. They were all waiting, holding their breath, to see what would happen next. Everything was now in place: the plugs were plugged in and the switches were flicked on and the buttons were flashing and the humming things were humming, and the machine was basically all set and ready to go. Pippa slowly put out a hand to touch it – all those red, blue and yellow buttons looked so inviting – but her new friend jumped in front of her.

'NO!' shouted Smug, making Pippa jump so high she almost leaped right out of her stripy tights. 'I'm sorry to startle you,' said the pug more quietly, 'but you absolutely must not touch anything until I have explained exactly how the invention works.'

Dash cocked an ear at this. 'Oh really?' he said. 'So you're saying this machine is *dangerous*? In that case, Mrs Fudge, I strongly recommend that—'

'Dash, dear, please allow them to demonstrate,' said Mrs Fudge.

Smug's wrinkly face wrinkled up even further, into something resembling a smile. 'Thank you, Mrs Fudge,' he said. Then, turning to Pippa, 'Firstly, I shall require a model.'

'A model what?' asked Pippa, who was feeling giddy with confusion and excitement. 'A model citizen?' she went on. 'A model aeroplane? A model village? A model train?'

Tallulah waved her hands to silence Pippa. 'No, no!' she chortled. 'He means a *model* – you know, like a fashion model! We'll need someone to sit in the chair here –' she indicated where she had fixed one of the twirly-whirly chairs into the machine.

Smug nodded. 'And then I will ask what style *madam* requires – I believe that is the wording one uses in hair salons, is it not?'

'And what would *you* know?' Dash muttered. 'By the looks of Tallulah's hair, she has never set foot in a hair salon before today.'

The pug narrowed his eyes. 'As I was saying, who would like to sit in the chair so that I may demonstrate the usefulness of my machine?' He looked around the expectant group.

'Not me!' said Tallulah. 'I am very fond of my style just the way it is.' She patted her bouncy red cloud of hair to show just how fond of it she was.

Dash let out a snort.

'Of course, Tally, of course,' said Smug. 'But what about Pippa?'

Pippa shook her head nervously. The last time she had let anyone near her hair, it had been a very painful experience.

'I shall be your model,' said Mrs Fudge. Everyone turned to look at the little old lady.

 92

She was holding her chin in the air, her face flushed with excitement.

Smug jumped up on to a chair next to the machine so that he was closer in height to the old lady and said, 'We were hoping for a . . . er . . . shall we say, less mature candidate?'

Dash immediately threw himself at the chair Smug was on, yelping and snarling. 'How dare you be so rude about Mrs Fudge!' he began. He did not get very far though, due to his legs being so under-long. He stood up on his hind paws, snapping and growling, while Smug sat quietly on the chair, smiling in a satisfied way.

Pippa noticed that Mrs Fudge's face had fallen and she was not looking so excited any more.

'I – I am sure that the machine will work on anyone,' said Tallulah.

'Well, I should jolly well hope so,' said Dash. 'Our customers are all ages, shapes and sizes, so if your machine cannot cope, then I think you should take it away right now—'

93

'Hello, darlin's! What is all de racket and hullaballoo around here dis fine afternoon?'

'Raphael!' cried Dash, immediately rushing over to greet his friend. 'Thank goodness you're here. Someone sane — at last.'

10

Raphael Is Bowled Over

'Oh my!' said the postie, staring at the shiny buttons and flashing lights. 'That is some con-trap-tion you have there, man!'

'It is a hair-cutting-and-styling machine,' said Tallulah proudly. 'We invented it to help Mrs Fudge here, who is in need of an extra pair of hands.'

'And so she is, darlin', and so she is,' said Raphael, clapping the girl on the shoulder. 'Oh! You must be de Foghorn girl!' he added. 'Am I right or am I right? I has been past your house a few times. Strange though, cos I has not had any post for you yet,' he added, looking suddenly quite serious. 'And I hasn't seen your gran'father either. Is you all right in that big old hotchpotch of a house, young lady? Every time I pass by, all I hears is funny noises, a-whirrin' and a-clickin' away.'

Tallulah reeled somewhat under the weight of Raphael's hand. 'Yes, er, quite all right, thank you,' she said.

Dash watched her closely and glanced at Smug too. He was certain he saw the little pug shake his head firmly as if warning Tallulah to say no more.

Everyone shuffled and waited for someone else to speak. An atmosphere of awkwardness had descended on the company like a chilly morning mist.

'So,' said the postie, finally breaking the silence, 'has any o' you had a go at this new machine yet?'

'Mrs Fudge volunteered,' said Dash, 'but it seems that she is not the sort of model we are looking for.' He shot a steely-eyed look at Smug, who made a big show of settling his spectacles back on to his tiny nose and washing his front paws.

'Will you let me try it?' asked Raphael, his eyes shining. 'I has been tinkin' that I is needin' a new look, Mrs Fudge darlin'. Maybe now is de time!' He rubbed his hands together.

'I am sure we could come up with something suitable,' said Smug smoothly.

Raphael whirled around. He peered at the two dogs. 'Dash, is you teasin' me? Pretendin' to speak for this cute li'l fella here?' he said, pointing at Smug.

'Ah, thank you for the compliment,' said Smug. He lowered his head in a modest manner.

'Goodness to mercy, I is goin' crazy!' Raphael cried.

'No, no, you're not,' said Pippa.

'This is fascinating,' murmured Tallulah. 'Another human who can understand Smug. What an intriguing place this town is turning out to be . . .'

Pippa drew herself up tall, and putting on her

most important-sounding tone of voice she said, 'Tally says only special people can understand Smug. And we must be special because we can understand Dash,' she said.

'Humpf!' said Dash. 'Why can't you understand all the other dogs around here then?'

Tallulah cleared her throat. 'It may have something to do with the fact that the other canines have nothing interesting to say.'

Dash lowered his head in the doggy equivalent of a blush. 'Oh, er. Yes, that is rather likely,' he mumbled.

'Well!' said Raphael. He looked from pug to dachshund and then back to the machine. 'What a day dis is turnin' out to be!'

'So it is,' said Smug impatiently. 'Now, shall we proceed with the demonstration?'

Raphael carefully lowered himself into the twirly-whirly chair. This was tricky because of his long legs and his rollerblades. The postie had to fold himself up like an umbrella to fit in under

 98

the machine as it hung low over the seat.

Smug waited until Raphael was comfortable. Then he said, 'What will it be today, sir?'

'Oh, I tink jus' a trim,' said Raphael, sounding distinctly more nervous now that he was in the chair.

The pug nodded to Tallulah, who turned a few wheels, flicked some levers and pressed a green button. Then Tallulah lowered the visor over Raphael's face ('To stop bits of hair flying into your mouth and eyes,' she explained) and pressed a large red button. Immediately two white-gloved hands sprang out from little doors in the sides of the machine. One hand picked up a loop of Raphael's black hair and the other whipped out some scissors from another small door. Then SNIP-SNIP-SNIPPETY-SNIP! The hands went into a whirlwind of activity, chopping and trimming and clipping away.

Pippa's stomach did a backflip as she watched the scissors slice through Raphael's hair. I do hope this

machine knows what it is doing, she thought.

Raphael's face meanwhile had gone from nervous to uneasy through to downright scared as he saw great long strands of his own hair flying through the air.

'I – I tink that be enough for me today,' he cried out, his eyes wide.

Tallulah stepped forward and pressed a yellow button and the hands froze in mid-air. The whizzing and whirring noises stopped as well. Then, quick as a bolt of lightning, the gloved hands zipped back into the doors in the side of the machine.

Raphael struggled out of the seat and glanced anxiously at himself in the mirror. He smoothed his hands over his scalp as he took in his reflection.

It was fair to say that a new look had been achieved. His hair was short and spiky and there was a magnificently inscribed letter 'R' shaved into the back of his scalp. Pippa held up a hand

mirror so
that Raphael
could
inspect
himself
from all
angles.

The salon
was deathly
quiet. Even
Muffles
did not
stir, purr
or twitch a whisker.

Please let him be happy! Pippa prayed, her fingers
crossed behind her back.

'Well!' said Raphael finally.

He stepped back, gave a slow twirl on his
rollerblades, then stood looking at himself again.
A smile crept into the corners of his mouth.
Then he smacked his thigh and boomed, 'I is

lookin' gooooooood!' His mouth stretched into the widest of smiles. 'I is lookin' handsome, man!' he added.

Everyone let out the breath they had been holding and there was a scattering of anxious laughter.

'Yeah!' Raphael continued, with a little pirouette of joy. 'You, Miss Tallulah and Mr Smug Pug, are de business, with your mar-vell-ous in-ven-tion! Mrs Fudge, they has read my mind! I would not have been able to describe exactly what I wanted for me new look, but the machine has got it right. Almost as though it has read me mind!'

'How interesting . . .' began Tallulah.

'Ahem!' Smug coughed loudly. 'I *am* pleased.'

'Not as pleased as me, man! I is very, *very* happy. I tink you has found your new pair o' hands, Mrs F.'

Pippa cheered and gave Raphael a high-five while Mrs Fudge congratulated Smug and Tallulah.

'Genius!' she said. 'Absolute genius!'

Only Dash could be heard to mutter in disgust, 'But you don't look like Raphael any more! And I would hardly call that "just a trim". What would your lady customers say to such a drastic restyle, Mrs Fudge? Have you thought of that?'

No one was listening though.

Raphael was so thrilled with his new look that he declared he would help to advertise the incredible hairstyling machine.

'I will speed off t'rough de town right away, me darlin's!' he cried, looking at himself this way and that in the mirror. 'You know how the Crumblies like me to keep them posted! Well, that's what I'll do! You will have de whole town clamouring at the door to try out this ting, Mrs Fudge!'

'Yes, well, I'm not sure I need even *more* customers, Raphael dear,' said Mrs Fudge cautiously. 'And don't forget I have all the dogs to look after as well.'

'But that's just the point, madam,' said Smug, 'if

 104

you'll pardon me for butting in. Now that you have the machine, you can take on as many customers as you like. And,' he added, 'you will be rich beyond your wildest dreams.'

11

Marble Gets the Foghorn Treatment

Raphael was true to his word. Within the hour, the phone (which Pippa had remembered to plug back in) was ringing off the hook.

'Of course the first person to book was Marble,' said Pippa, rolling her eyes. 'How does she manage to always be at the front of any queue?'

'Who is Marble?' asked Smug.

'Marble Wainwright,' said Mrs Fudge. 'She's – how should I put it . . . ?'

'Our grumpiest client,' Dash said, with some relish. 'She is *extremely* difficult to please. In fact, I do not think anyone has ever managed to please Marble. It's not all fun and games here, you see, Smug,' he added. 'Some of our customers are distinctly tricky, and it takes an experienced hand to know how to deal with them.'

'Oh, don't you worry about us,' said Smug. 'We are used to dealing with tricky people. Do you remember the time we delivered the lawn-cutting machine to that old major-general in Little Snitting on the Wold?' he said, turning to Tallulah.

'Oh my goodness!' squealed Tallulah. 'Do I ever!' She burst into giggles at the memory.

'He was—!'

'Wasn't he!'

Dash coughed loudly. 'I'm sorry to break up your cosy little reminiscences,' he said, 'but I think we should be tidying this place up before Marble and the others arrive, don't you?' He shot a glance at the wires, flexes and plugs, towels, bottles and pots of lotions that were strewn around the salon.

'Oh goodness, yes,' said Mrs Fudge. She looked flustered.

But – DRIIIINNNG!

'Oh no, Marble's here already!' cried Pippa. She

sped round the salon gathering up armfuls of towels
and chucking them at Tallulah, who merely whirled
around on the spot shouting uselessly, 'What do I
do with these?'

Dash raised his eyes to the heavens and gave a
small snort (which if he had been a human, would
have come out as a sort of tutting noise).

Smug cried, 'Over here, Tally. Quick, stow them
behind the counter.'

Mrs Fudge was hurriedly pushing hairdryers and
straighteners into the nearest drawer, and Pippa
meanwhile had grabbed a broom and was sweeping
the bottles of shampoo, conditioner and hair dye
into a corner.

DRIIIINNNNGG! DRIIIIIIIINNNNNGG!

Pippa took a running leap over the two dogs
and skittered out of the salon to reach Marble
before she could press the bell again. She flung
the door open and the grumpy old woman
pushed straight past Pippa, throwing her ugly
black tea-cosy hat and her lumpy sack of a coat

at Tallulah, who was right behind her.

'Hello, Marble,' said Pippa. She stood with her hands on her hips, challenging Marble to look her in the eye and be polite.

Marble sniffed and grunted, 'At last. What did you keep me waiting for? I hope old Semolina is ready for us. We haven't got time to hang about.' And with that she marched off, dragging her little Welsh terrier, Snooks, behind her.

'Goodness me, what an exceptionally discourteous woman,' said Tallulah. 'Not very polite,' she explained, when Pippa looked at her quizzically.

'Oh. Yes. Well, that's Marble,' said Pippa. 'If she had a family motto it would be "Why be polite and nice if you can be rude and horrible?"' She pulled a face. 'But her dog, Snooks, is totally cute,' she added.

'I noticed,' said Tallulah, as she followed Marble's big wobbly bottom down the hallway and into the salon.

'Oh my lawks!' cried Marble, as she stood in the doorway with an expression of terror on her face. 'What on earth is that horrible robot doing in the middle of your salon, Mrs Fudge?'

'You may well ask,' said Dash. (But of course Marble could not understand him.)

Mrs Fudge gave him a stern look, then came bustling over from behind the counter, where she had been checking through her list of appointments. 'Marble, dear! How are you today?'

'I'm not so good, as it happens. I've got a chill and an ache and I can't *tell* you about my legs. But I feel even so much more worse now that I've

110

clapped eyes on that monster!' she wailed.

Mrs Fudge laid a soothing hand on her customer's arm. 'Marble, this "monster", as you put it, is far from horrible. This is the machine that Raphael has been telling everyone about – the one you wanted to see! And I can assure you it is the most marvellous invention. It is going to change the face of hairdressing forever.'

'I don't want to change my face,' Marble whimpered.

'Are you sure?' muttered Tallulah, catching Pippa's eye and setting them both off into a prolonged bout of silent laughter.

Mrs Fudge looked at them from over the top of her half-moon spectacles and said, 'Girls, why don't you make a fresh pot of tea while I get Marble and Snooks settled?'

'But it doesn't take two of us to—' Pippa squeaked, wiping tears of laughter from her eyes.

'I think it might. Just this once,' insisted Mrs Fudge.

111

Pippa glanced at Tallulah and shrugged helplessly and the pair did as they were told. 'She always does this when she wants to get rid of me,' Pippa grumbled.

When they came back in Marble was in the chair with the Foghorns' machine in place over her head.

'I wonder how she persuaded the old trout to try it,' Tallulah whispered.

'Oh, Marble doesn't like to miss out on anything,' Pippa told her. 'I expect Mrs Fudge told her that *everyone* in Crumbly-under-Edge was desperate to have their hair done with it, and that if she did not want her appointment, there were a lot of other people who would gladly take her place.'

'So, what are you after today, Marble?' asked Mrs Fudge. She always rather dreaded Marble coming in, because the dumpy woman always expected Mrs Fudge to make her look like a supermodel.

'I should like my hair to be very long, very straight, and very, very blonde,' Marble snapped.

'Like that terribly elegant Italian fashion-designer person,' she added. 'Whatshername, y'know, Donatella Panettone.'

Mrs Fudge said slowly, 'All right.'

'Errr-raaoow!' commented Muffles, which was the closest she ever came to a snigger.

And snigger she might, for Marble's hair was the very opposite of what she had asked for: extremely short, very curly and very, very black (because the last time she had come for an appointment, that is what she had asked for).

'The thing is, Marble dear,' Mrs Fudge began carefully, 'I am not sure that even the machine can manage that in a half-hour appointment. It would involve putting hair extensions in. You'll need a few hours to achieve that look.'

'Hours?' Marble gasped in outrage. 'I haven't got *hours*. I thought this machine was supposed to be super-speedy. And anyway, I think it's very rude to imply that it would take *hours* to make me look lovely.'

113

'Hmm,' muttered Pippa. 'More like days or weeks.'

'Or even millennia,' remarked Smug.

'Certainly years,' squeaked Pippa.

'That's what Smug meant,' said Tallulah, giggling.

'What's that?' snapped Marble, turning to shoot a dirty look in the girls' direction.

'Pippa said it would be a shame to cover your lovely ears,' said Tallulah, choking on her laughter.

'Marble, I did not mean to offend you,' said Mrs Fudge in a soothing voice. 'Let's do a little experiment, shall we? I'll programme the machine to see what it can do, and if the result isn't what you wanted, I'll book you in for a restyling tomorrow, free of charge. How does that sound?'

Now Marble was always one for a bargain. She was a meanie and could not resist anything that was free. So that did it.

'It will do, I suppose,' she said grudgingly. 'Well, get a move on, can't you? I haven't got all day.'

So Mrs Fudge bent down and very quietly and

swiftly consulted Smug. Then, coming back to the machine, she muttered to herself, 'Red button, blue lever, green switch,' and pressed and flicked and clicked and . . .

WHOOSH! The machine surged into life; the white-gloved hands popped out of the little doors, flexing their robotic muscles and wiggling their mechanical fingers. Then one of them whisked out a small, unnoticed drawer from the side of the machine. The drawer was full of golden blonde tresses, which the hand delved into. Both hands proceeded to go into overdrive, plaiting and tweaking and stretching and knotting and weaving. They moved so fast over Marble's head that you could not make out what they were doing. Everyone, most of all Mrs Fudge, hoped that they were doing exactly what Marble wanted. For if Marble was not satisfied with the results, the news would be around the whole of Crumbly-under-Edge in a matter of hours, and then no one would ever come to Chop 'n' Chat again.

Then as suddenly as they had begun, the hands stopped their frenzied attack on Marble's head. They shot into the air as though to salute the horrible old woman's reflection, and then quick as a flash they zoomed back into the little doors and snapped out of sight.

Mrs Fudge and Pippa could not quite see the results of the makeover as the machine was close up to the mirror and Marble was leaning forward too, making heavy breathing noises through her nose like an outsized whistling kettle.

'Well!' she exclaimed finally.

'What do you – what do you think, Marble?' Mrs Fudge ventured.

There was a long pause in which every tick of the clock and every gentle purr from the now sleeping Muffles could be heard.

Then, 'Ahem,' said Marble. She paused. 'I have to say, I am . . . hmmm . . .' she paused again. She twisted her tight little lips. (No one could tell what that facial expression meant. It could have been

 116

a frown of concentration; it could have been a grimace of disgust. Potatoey faces such as Marble's are so difficult to read.)

She pushed back the visor and began awkwardly to extract herself from the chair. Pippa rushed to help, pulling the machine back so that Marble could hop down.

The vision that met everyone's eyes was astounding.

Marble looked beautiful!

She had a full head of the most gleamingly blonde locks you have ever seen. They shone like spun gold, as though fairies had made it from gossamer or whatever fairies would use to make blonde hair with. But it wasn't so much the hair that knocked the breath out of everyone. For somehow, in that instant of lifting the visor, Marble's face had undergone a magnificent change. It was glowing rather than trout-like, and her nose was now buttony rather than potatoey. Her tiny currant-ish eyes were gleaming like bright jewels and her normally puckered mouth was wider and shinier and turned up at the corners as if she was—

'Smiling? . . . Are you – are you really *smiling*, Marble?' stammered Mrs Fudge.

'I do believe I am!' said Marble, in a twinkly voice.

That's what's so different about her, thought Pippa. It's not the hair at all. It's the fact that Marble Wainwright is smiling!

'I have to say, Semolina,' said Marble, using the name Mrs Fudge hated so much, 'I am, for once, more than a little bit satisfied. In fact, I am the happiest I can ever remember being. It's as if the machine has read my mind!'

'Oh!' said Tallulah.

'Grr!' said Smug.

'What's the matter?' Dash asked, but Marble was talking over the top of the girl and her pug.

'Yes! This is amazing,' she was saying. 'I shall be recommending this machine to everyone I know in Crumbly-under-Edge. These Foghorns are obviously geniuses. I should like to meet your grandfather, young lady,' she said to Tallulah. 'He clearly knows more about what a woman wants than, I'm sorry to say, Mrs Fudge does.'

Raphael had been under strict instructions not to mention Smug's role in the invention, for the obvious reason that no one would believe a dog could have invented anything.

'Hey!' protested Dash. 'You might look all lovely with your new hair and that smile on your face, but there's no need to be—'

'What's the mutt yapping about now?' said Marble, her smile fading rapidly.

Pippa scooped him up and nuzzled him against

119

her cheek. 'Shh,' she whispered. 'You have to admit this machine must be marvellous if it can make Marble Wainwright happy.'

But Dash merely growled.

That does it, he thought. The next chance I get, I'm going to have a snoop around the Foghorns' place and find out as much as I can about this family. There is something fishy going on – I just *know* it!

12

Astonishing Transformations

Marble's experience with the hairdressing machine
soon set tongues wagging in Crumbly-under-Edge.
Customers flocked to the salon to have their own
'Foghorn Treatment', as it had become known.

And the funny thing was that Marble had not
needed to brag as she usually did. One look at
her was enough to set people chattering about
'miracles' and 'astonishing transformations'. People
kept coming up to her and crying out, 'Excuse
me, but I must say your hair is simply marvellous!
Where *did* you get it done?' And they were always
shocked with the answer. Not so much because
Marble told them she had been to Chop 'n' Chat,
but because they had not realized it was Marble

Wainwright they were talking to!

Coral Jones was a prime example. 'Oh, goodness!' she twittered when she saw it was Marble she was standing next to in a queue in the butcher's one morning. 'I – I didn't recognize – that is, you look so different – that is, I don't mean to imply that you don't usually look so—'

'It's all right, Coral. I know what you mean,' said Marble, simpering and batting her eyelashes. 'I don't usually look so beautiful. I'm not a fool. I know I am a bit of a potato-face. But this machine, well, it's changed my life! I've never been happier. You have to try it, Coral.'

So of course Coral did try it. And then Mrs Prim did, and then Millicent Beadle and then Mrs Peach. And they all looked so gorgeously glamorous that they too were soon walking around shouting the machine's praises from the rooftops (not literally, you understand, as that would be terribly dangerous and ever so annoyingly noisy too).

And then there were the boys who had seen

 122

Raphael's new style. Kurt immediately rushed to book an appointment to have his blue Mohican changed to a shaved, cropped style with a jagged 'K' carved into the back of his hair. There were a few wispy blue bits left in the spiky sticky-uppy part on top of his head, but Kurt was quite pleased with that. (Mrs Fudge was also very relieved that she no longer had to separate six eggs to get the whites to make Kurt's Mohican stand up straight. She had always complained that she did not know what to do with so many yolks. 'There's only so much ice cream and custard an old lady can get through,' she used to say.)

Now you might think that this is where the story should end. After all, everyone was happy, Mrs Fudge had more help than she could have dreamed of, she had *two* wonderful assistants who got on like a house on fire *and* more satisfied customers than ever. And of course Pippa felt she had done better than anyone, for she had a brand-new friend, two lovely dogs to spend all her spare time with and school was not a chore any more.

However, if you were hoping for
a short read, I am sorry to have
to disappoint you, for I am
afraid we have not reached the
'happily ever after' part yet.

You're telling ME!

For a start, Dash was far from feeling happily
ever after. He could not see why Smug the pug was
good news for anyone, particularly himself.

'That pug lives up to his name at least one hundred
times a day,' he grumbled under his breath, as Smug
sent him off on another errand. 'He has walked in
here and made himself top dog! My home is not my
own any more. But none of the others can see it.'

And that was partly true.

ONE
MILLION
PER CENT
TRUE

It was one
million per
cent true!

Actually, I think you'll find that, technically, it is impossible to have one million per cent as, strictly speaking, 'per cent' means 'out of one hundred' and—

Oh, do be quiet.

As I was saying, before I was so *rudely interrupted*, it was partly true. As charming and as helpful as Smug was, he did seem remarkably pleased with himself. To make matters worse,

Smug was also quite bossy. He did seem to take rather a lot of pleasure in barking out his commands so that Pippa and Mrs Fudge knew how to use the machine (for even Tallulah did not entirely understand how it worked). And he especially enjoyed barking out commands to Dash, which was extremely annoying for the little dachshund.

'Pippa and I were once a team,' Dash was frequently heard to grumble. 'And now she has got Tallulah and I am thrown together with Mr Bossy-Boots and Mrs Fudge is too busy to notice.'

That was the other thing: Mrs Fudge was run off her feet. Again! She had begun by being nicely busy. Then when Mrs Prim and Coral and all the others had spread the word further afield Mrs Fudge found that she had become *very* busy. But pretty soon Chop 'n' Chat had become what can only be described as *too* busy.

The trouble was the customers wanted their appointments at once because they suddenly

could not bear to be the only person in Crumbly-
under-Edge who was not sporting the latest
Foghorn makeover. This meant she had queues
of people waiting, needing tea and cakes and
sympathy too, and of course they all brought
their dogs and wanted them pampered while they
waited.

'Pippa, dear,' said Mrs Fudge one afternoon. 'I
wonder if you could take over. I feel quite worn
out. I am going to have to put my feet up.'

Pippa could not believe her ears. Normally Mrs
Fudge liked to keep an eye on Pippa's jobs in the
salon, just in case she got 'carried away with the
scissors'.

'Are you sure?' Pippa asked.

'Yes, yes. The machine runs itself once you've
pressed a few buttons, so you can get on with the
dogs, and I am sure Tallulah will know what to do
in the kitchen,' said Mrs Fudge, yawning. 'I'm just
going to have forty winks. I'll be upstairs if you
need me, but I'm sure you won't.'

127

Pippa was delighted. 'I'm sure I won't need any help at all!' she trilled, and skipped off to the salon to make sure everything was in order.

How little did she know.

13

Pippa Takes Control

You could say that the trouble started when Pippa was asked to take over. But really I suppose that is a trifle unfair, for if Mrs Fudge had not accepted Smug's machine into her establishment in the first place, none of what followed would have happened.

However, there can be no denying that the trouble properly started when Pippa called a meeting to discuss how things would be handled while Mrs Fudge was having a break.

'Let's face it,' said Pippa, 'Mrs Fudge needs more than forty winks. She needs about a million and forty. If not forty million.'

'All right, all right,' said Dash. 'We get your

point. So let's get rid of the infernal contraption and go back to doing things the old-fashioned way. For one thing, we're neglecting the dogs.'

'That's where Smug comes in,' said Pippa, her turquoise eyes flashing with excitement.

'Of course, I should've known,' snapped Dash.

'What have you got in mind?' asked the little pug, taking off his spectacles and licking them thoroughly clean.

'I was wondering . . .' said Pippa. She paused and caught Tallulah's eye. 'Smug, do you remember the bath tub you showed me at your house? We-e-ell . . . when Raphael came to have his hair cut, you *did* say that you could invent a dog-grooming machine if we wanted it.'

'That is correct,' said Smug. Dash snarled but Smug ignored him. 'Go on.'

'I think it would be *brilliant* if you could invent such a machine for the dogs at Chop 'n' Chat,' Pippa said. 'That way we would have more time to care for the customers and listen to their chatter.

And if Mrs Fudge wanted to take things easy and concentrate on baking and tea-making, she would be free to do that.'

Smug bowed his head. 'I think I could turn my paw to something suitable,' he said.

Dash's snarling increased in volume.

Smug glared at him, then said to Pippa, 'As it happens, I have been playing around with a new idea in the Inventionary. It needs a bit more work, but it's ninety-nine per cent there.'

'Oh nonononono!' Dash exploded. 'You can't be serious about this idea, can you, Pippa? I mean, think of what you are doing! You are letting machines take over! What will it be next? A machine to deliver all the post so that poor Raphael is out of a job?'

'Actually that's not a bad idea,' Tallulah commented. 'He could do with a rest now and again. He does whizz around a lot.'

'He LIKES "whizzing around"!' snapped Dash. 'Just as we *like* caring for our customers ourselves

131

instead of pushing buttons and pulling levers. And just *look* at what you have done to Mrs Fudge! She is more worn out than ever and her house is not her own any more. Her business has taken over her life, and her at age it just is not fair . . .'

As Dash went on and on, Smug tapped Pippa on the knee and slid her a little note. She glanced at it. It said:

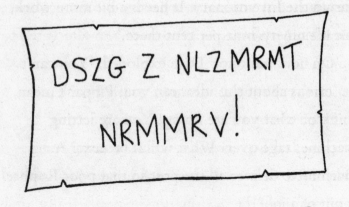

DSZG Z NLZMRMT

NRMMRV!

It's that code, Pippa thought. Now, she was not as brainy as Tallulah, so it took her a few minutes to work it out, but luckily Dash was still ranting and raving, so by the time he had finished, she had decoded it.

'Hee hee hee!' She burst into a torrent of giggles.

Hackles immediately went up the length of Dash's back, making him look like a ruffled feather duster. 'I don't see that there is ANYTHING to laugh about!' he barked.

'Moaning minnie!' Pippa chortled, repeating the last two words of the coded message (work it out for yourself if you don't believe me). 'Too right – moaning MINI-ature dachshund!' she whispered to Smug.

'It is very rude to whisper,' snarled Dash.

Pippa chewed the insides of her mouth to stop the laughter and said, 'Dash, you are being ridiculous. Come on – we need to help Smug by giving him all the information he needs. Tally, grab a piece of paper and we'll jot down everything we can think of about pooch-pampering to help Smug finish the design.'

And so the two girls sat at the kitchen table and brainstormed what would be needed to create the ultimate Foghorn Pooch-Pamperer, and Smug nodded or frowned at their suggestions and took notes and chipped in with his own comments on what he might need.

Meanwhile poor Dash sat in his dog basket by the stove and sulked and plotted and grumbled to himself.

This is no good, he thought. I am wasting time by sitting around feeling sorry for myself. I need to take action. I am going to sniff my way over to where the Foghorns live. I shall do some snooping around. I would like to take a look at this latest so-called 'invention' of Smug's before he gets to wow everyone with his cleverness again.

And with that he tiptoed out of the kitchen, zipped out of the back door and was away without anyone noticing he had gone.

'So we need a shampooer and a dryer, of course,' Pippa was saying. 'But different breeds need different settings. For example, you can't use the

 134

same amount of shampoo on a chihuahua as you do on a St Bernard.'

'Elementary,' said Smug.

'What?' Pippa jumped. That was the word Dash used when they were problem-solving. She glanced anxiously at the miniature dachshund to see if he had noticed, but Dash, of course, was no longer there. Pippa heaved a sigh of relief. He must have nipped out into the garden, she thought.

Tallulah chipped in, 'Yes, it is obvious you

135

cannot use the same amount of product on such vastly differing surface areas,' she said. 'I had already thought of that.'

'However,' said Smug, scribbling away, 'we should make certain of our calculations in any case. We don't want to get the quantities wrong.' He had soon covered the entire kitchen table in paper filled with what looked to Pippa to be incredibly complex sums.

At least the actual table hasn't been scribbled on this time, she thought.

Eventually Smug sat back in his chair and gestured to his calculations. 'Tell me if you spot any inconsistencies, Tally,' he said.

Tallulah's mouth was twisted in concentration as she scanned the pages. 'Hmm, I see,' she said. 'There are many things to be taken into account.'

Pippa felt a twinge of worry. I hope they know what they are doing, she thought.

Tallulah looked at her. 'Smug will check through the sums as he builds the machine to make sure that

 136

there is a different setting for each breed. He has possibly not considered every single type of dog. We'll just need to run a few experiments at home first.'

'OK,' Pippa said. 'So then there's things like clipping,' she told them. 'Some breeds need it, some don't, and some need to be done by hand rather than with an electric clipper. Border terriers, for example: they look better if they've been hand-stripped.'

'Ouch,' said Smug. 'That sounds painful.'

'Not at all.' Pippa shook her head. 'Trust me. You just use a special stripping knife, or you can even use your fingers. The dogs who have it done actually like it.'

'If you're sure,' said Smug doubtfully. 'I can attach a tool for that. I will put in some mechanical hands, such as the ones that are used in the hairdressing machine.'

And so the conversation went on, with the three friends discussing in detail how to put together a

137

device that would do all the jobs Mrs Fudge and Pippa usually did, but at twice the speed.

'This is going to be brilliant, if I do say so myself,' sighed Smug.

14

Dash Does Some Detecting

Meanwhile, Dash was making swift progress in finding his way to the Foghorns' place. He had run out of Mrs Fudge's garden and around to the front of the house and was already down Liquorice Drive.

'I shall follow Tallulah's and Smug's scents and track down their house,' he said to himself. 'It shouldn't be too hard. That pug reeks of self-importance and Tallulah has a particularly pungent waft of Miss Clever-Two-Shoes about her.'

He put his long pointy nose to the ground and followed the niffs out to the main road that led into Crumbly-under-Edge. He had soon left the shops and the park behind him. Dogs he knew barked out greetings and asked him where he was going, but he did not hear them, he was concentrating so hard. He passed the neat rows of houses with their white picket fences in the newer part of town, and still the scents led him on.

Suddenly the Smuggy-puggy scent of pleased-with-himself-smugness and Tallulah's cleverness became overwhelming.

'If I didn't know for certain that they were still with Pippa, I would say they were both right here,' he said aloud.

He chased his tail round and round as he sniffed and sniffed at the powerful odours. Then at last he looked up ahead and realized that in his race to follow the scent he had taken himself all the way to the other side of the town. It was an area he was unfamiliar with. He certainly did not recognize the gate he had stopped at: it was rusty and hanging off its hinges at an odd angle, and it creaked noisily as it swung in the chilly April breeze.

 140

'This place looks as though it has been empty for years,' Dash mused as he looked down the path, which was overgrown with weeds. The front door had been painted white once upon a time, but now the paint was peeling off it and the brass knocker and the letter box were dull and dirty with age. (None of this had made the slightest impression on Pippa when she had visited. She had been far too

excited about the scooter-mobile and about visiting her new friends' home.)

The door was open a tiny crack, Dash noted with puzzlement.

He tiptoed around the side of the house to investigate at the back. 'It is odd that I cannot seem to pick up any other scents,' he said to himself. 'Surely I should be able to sniff out Tallulah's grandfather as well . . . unless . . . unless he doesn't exist!'

Dash sat back on his haunches and pondered. 'What wouldn't I give for a couple of nice crunchy bones to help me think through this conundrum,' he said. 'This is another one of those two-bone problems. But there's no way of getting a nice crunchy bone around here, so I shall just have to rely on good old common sense.' He closed his eyes, all the better to concentrate. 'Let me think . . . No one, not even Raphael, has seen hide nor hair of this grandfather person. And yet Tallulah must have *someone* to look after her. Even

I know that Smug, however marvellous he is, is a dog, and therefore cannot look after a human child. Unless – oh no!' Dash shivered. 'What if *Smug* is her grandfather? What if he is a spy of some kind and has invented a way of turning himself into a dog so that he can go undercover?' Dash felt a ripple of panic run through him. 'I have to get back to the salon and warn Pippa,' he told himself. 'But she'll want proof. If I don't bring proof, she will just tell me off again for making everything up and being jealous.'

He was really feeling very nervous now about what he might find, but he knew he had to be brave. 'I am doing this for Pippa and for Mrs Fudge,' he told himself as he crept along to the back door.

As luck would have it, there was an old cat flap installed there, which was just the right size for a miniature dachshund to crawl through. He poked his nose through first and had a good sniff around.

'Mmm,' he said. 'Still not much in the way of

new aromas – nothing to suggest a grandfatherly presence.'

(If you want to know what a grandfather smells like, you will have to ask Dash, as I have no idea.) Next Dash summoned up his courage and leaped daintily through the cat flap.

He was as shocked as Pippa had been by the state of the place. 'It's a good job I have such an amazing sense of smell!' the little dog exclaimed. 'My eyes are not much good to me here.' Being the short pooch he was, he could not see beyond the furniture and the stacks of books and papers. He scuttled along to the Inventionary, where another machine seemed to be in the early stages of development. There was less clutter on the floor in this room, so Dash was able to take in the complicated contraption with its ropes and levers and coils and springs and bells and whistles.

'What on earth is this going to be for?' Dash wondered aloud.

He decided to jump on to a low chair and from

 144

there to a table so that he could get a closer look at the invention.

Not that this gave him any clearer an idea. He did, however, find a piece of paper on which was scrawled the most perplexing arrangement of letters:

'He *must* be a spy!' Dash said. 'Only spies use codes. And this looks exactly like code to me' (which just goes to show exactly how clever he was).

TLMV LFG ZTZRM. WL MLG GLFXS!

clever

Why, thank you!

You're welcome.

But sadly he was
not quite clever
enough to work
out how to break
the code.

HEY!

Well, you
weren't,
were you?

blushes NO . . .

And so he was left none the wiser. However, he did
think it might be a clue.

'If this doesn't prove the grandfather is a tricky
piece of work, I don't know what does,' he said.

Then he picked up the piece of paper and held it gently in his mouth. 'I will take it back to Chop 'n' Chat as evidence.'

He then eyed the apparatus in front of him and thought about touching it to see what would happen. He stared up at the huge muddle of levers and ropes and wheels and attachments which surrounded a very ordinary-looking chair.

The contraption was monstrous! If you had peeked through the window, you would have seen how small and vulnerable the little pooch was next to the device towering over him. But Dash was a brave dog. He carefully dropped the piece of paper he had been holding and went up to the machine. It smelt of oil and metal and not much else. He stepped back and noticed there was a very small lever just within reach of his nose. His curiosity overcame his nerves and he gently nudged the lever. Then, oh dear . . .

ZOOM! CLICK! WHIRR!

Two hands appeared from nowhere and held him

in a vice-like grip. They lifted him from the ground
and plonked him on to the chair.

'Ouch!' shouted Dash.

Whirr, click, SQUELCH!

A huge object that looked like a sink plunger
was lowered over Dash's head and fastened itself

to his scalp with a nasty sucking noise.

'Argh!' yelled Dash. He wriggled in vain to free himself.

Then the whirring and the clicking increased in volume and a ticking noise started up somewhere behind him. If Dash had known anything about computers, he might have said that it sounded like paper coming out of a printer. But he was a dog and knew nothing of such things. In any case, he was far too upset by now to be thinking much beyond, 'GET ME OUT OF HERE!'

Then something very odd happened. The noises all stopped at once. The sink-plunger-sucker thing removed itself from Dash's head (unfortunately taking rather a lot of his lovely red fur with it) and the hands let go of him. He was about to leap for safety when he heard another ticking, clicking noise – and then he froze.

A long streamer of paper, like loo roll, had come flying through the air. As it dropped in front of Dash, he caught sight of the words, 'Ouch!' and

'Argh!' and 'GET ME OUT OF HERE!'

That's funny, he thought. That's exactly what I was thinking when I was trapped in that thing. I really should investigate further—

But the very second that he thought this, something came out of the seat behind him, gave him an almighty push and propelled him out of the Inventionary and into the hall. The front door blew open ahead of him, and he was pushed out on to the drive, where he landed in a crumpled heap.

'That does it!' he whimpered, puffing and panting as he picked himself up. 'I am going back to tell Pippa right now what sort of dangerous nonsense her new friends are up to. We cannot possibly let them loose on the poochy population of Crumbly-under-Edge!'

15

The Pooch-Pampering Machine

But by the time Dash arrived back at Chop 'n' Chat,
Mrs Fudge and Pippa were having a cup of tea and
a natter in the kitchen, and Tallulah and Smug had
already left.

'Where are they?' he demanded. 'I have
something to say, and I want them to hear me
say it.'

'If by "they", you mean Smug and Tallulah,
they've gone home,' said Mrs Fudge.

'I bet they have,' began Dash. 'And I also bet I
know what they're up to—'

But Mrs Fudge interrupted excitedly, 'Pippa's
told me all about their idea for a dog-grooming
machine! It does sound marvellous . . .' Then she

tailed off and peered at the little pooch. 'Dash dear, are you feeling all right? You look as though you've been caught in a tornado – your fur is sticking up all over the place! What in heaven's name have you been up to?'

'THAT IS PRECISELY WHAT I WANT TO SPEAK TO SMUG AND TALLULAH ABOUT!' barked the miniature dachshund.

Muffles leaped in the air from her place on the window seat, howled in fury and left the room.

'Dash!' Pippa reprimanded. 'Please stop shouting and calm down.'

'But they are up to something – something devilish. Something devious. Something . . .' He broke off. He had run out of words beginning with D to describe exactly what Tallulah and Smug were up to.

'For goodness sake,' snapped Pippa, 'when are you going to stop being so ridiculously jealous?'

'Oh dear,' said Mrs Fudge. She took off her spectacles and rubbed her eyes. 'I have one of my headaches coming on. I'm going to have to have another lie-down.' She smiled wearily at Pippa. 'Can I leave things in your capable hands in the meantime? Mrs Prim's bringing George in for a trim.'

'Of course, Mrs Fudge! Why not have a proper snooze? You look as though you need it,' said Pippa. Then, under her breath to Dash, 'Now look what you've done.'

The old lady smiled gratefully. 'Thank you. Do please wake me when Tallulah and Smug come back with their invention, would you? Oh, and do the washing-up, dear, if you wouldn't mind.' And with that, she hobbled out, leaving Pippa and Dash alone in the kitchen.

Dash immediately scampered up to Pippa and put his paws on her knees. 'Listen,' he hissed. 'I've just been over to the Foghorns' and I've had first-hand experience of one of their inventions and I can tell you it is downright dangerous!'

'WHAT?' Pippa exclaimed. 'You broke into their house? What on *earth* have you been up to?'

Dash raised his hackles (at least, what few there were left after his adventure). He growled. 'Grr! I'll have you know that I was doing some detective work. The sort of detective work that you and I used to do – *together*.'

Pippa brushed Dash's paws from her knees with an irritable flick of her fingers. 'And I would have come with you, a) if you had asked me and b) if there was any need. Which there isn't! What exactly gives you the idea that we need to go sniffing around Tally and Smug's house? Nothing went wrong with the hairdressing machine, so why should there be anything wrong with the dog-grooming idea? You are just being grumpy and silly and—'

'Will you just LISTEN?' Dash interrupted. He jumped up again and put his paws on Pippa more firmly this time. 'That house is spooky. The grandfather is nowhere to be seen. There are coded messages lying around. And to top it all I have PROOF that there is something sinister going on. Listen to this: the invention I discovered in the house *read my mind*!'

'Hello! What a lot of noise. Is everything all right?' Tallulah was standing in the doorway surveying the scene.

'No, since you ask,' Dash said. 'Everything is far from all right.'

'Wow! You were quick,' said Pippa.

'Oh yes, the marvels of the super-fast scooter,' said Tallulah vaguely.

'Marvels indeed,' growled Dash.

'Ignore him,' said Pippa, standing up and stepping in front of the dachshund. 'He is a bit overexcited. We all are! We can't wait to see the new machine.'

'Well, that's splendid, because Smug is just setting it up in the salon right now. We towed it along behind us. He thinks it's fine and that no more adjustments are needed.'

'NO MORE ADJUST—?' barked Dash.

Pippa gave Dash a shove with her foot and said hurriedly, 'Let's see it then!' Just as she said this, the doorbell rang. 'That will be Mrs Prim,' she said. 'George can be our first customer to try the pooch-pampering machine!'

Mrs Prim's reaction to the invention could not have been more different from Dash's. She was overjoyed by the mere fact of being the first Crumbly to see it in action (mainly because it meant she had pipped Marble to the post).

Dash noticed that there was now a bath attached

to the apparatus, which confused him. Maybe this is not the horrific machine that pummelled and punched me then, he thought. But he felt a rumble of unease in his tummy nonetheless.

Mrs Prim was beaming as she took in the complicated design. 'My! It looks even more magnificent than the hairdressing invention!' she cooed. 'And luckily Georgie needs a good old trim, so – let's try it!' she announced. Her springer spaniel did look rather a mess. His ears were matted with burrs and mud and his usually glossy coat was knotty and tangled.

'He is a mucky pup, isn't he?' Mrs Prim giggled as she took in the looks on everyone's faces. 'I'm afraid that I let him go for a swim in the river just this once, seeing as he was coming for a shampoo anyway.'

Dash was feeling distinctly jumpy now. How can Pippa put an animal into a machine that she knows nothing about? he thought. I am certain this is going to end in tears. In any case, he went on grumbling to himself as he eyed the spaniel, I bet 'Georgie' will have seven fits if they try to strap him into that hideous invention.

George did indeed whimper as he was led towards it.

'Come along now, Georgie,' said Mrs Prim. 'Be a good boy for Mummy.'

Tallulah wheeled the machine into place and Pippa gently put George into the bath. Then Tallulah adjusted the shower fixture to the correct height. The machine immediately began to emit a loud whirring noise which George's whimpering matched in volume.

Then Smug barked, 'Green button!' The second Tallulah pressed the flashing light, the sink plunger descended and attached itself to George's head (but a lot more gently than it had done with poor Dash). The spaniel gave a louder whimper, but was drowned out by a ticking and whirring noise behind him. Then a streamer of paper shot out of the back of the machine with the word 'Biscuit!' on it.

Pippa gasped. 'What. . . ?'

Immediately the plunger was retracted and a hand appeared in front of George's nose with a tempting dog treat, which he gobbled up straight away. Then some soothing music was piped out of some speakers either side of the bath.

George had never looked calmer. In fact, Pippa thought, he looked almost hypnotized. His large brown eyes had grown larger and did not appear to be focused on anything. And his tongue was lolling rather stupidly out of the side of his mouth.

'Perfect,' Smug announced.

'Perfect?' cried Dash. 'The poor hound looks positively ill!' Although he had to admit to himself that this machine was, so far, behaving much better than he had feared it would.

'What an excitable pair,' commented Mrs Prim, watching Dash and Smug's exchange with

159

fascination. 'I do sometimes think it would be wonderful to be able to understand them, don't you? Although,' she added, not waiting for an answer, 'I have to say your clever machine *does* look as if it understands my darling Georgie. He seems very happy now that he's had that treat. Well, are you going to clean him up now?'

Pippa nodded. She could not bring herself to speak.

Tallulah stepped in. 'Wash first?' she asked briskly.

'Lovely,' said Mrs Prim.

'Blue button, then yellow, then orange lever,' commanded Smug.

Shampoo immediately poured out of a small spout on to George's matted coat, then two familiar white-gloved hands appeared from the sides of the contraption and began massaging the shampoo into George's fur. Soon he was a ball of white froth.

'Is – is he going to be all right?' faltered Mrs

Prim. Her bright, animated expression had faded and she was beginning to look a little worried. 'Only – I can't see him under all those bubbles. Mrs Fudge doesn't usually put so much shampoo on him.'

'Tell her I needed to use the Intense Wash setting,' said Smug. 'I have never seen such a filthy hound.'

'Rude!' exclaimed Dash. 'Just because you sit inside all day inventing things, Mr Clever-Clogs . . .'

Pippa raised her voice above Dash's growling and gave him a gentle prod with her toe. 'We have used a bit of extra product on George today, Mrs Prim,' she said. 'He was rather more dirty than normal.'

Mrs Prim blushed. 'Yes, yes. I am sure you know what you are doing. After all, I am very pleased with my new hair-do,' she said, patting her perfect blonde bob. 'If Georgie ends up looking even half as good I shall be pleased.'

161

'As will we, Mrs Prim,' added Tallulah.

We'll see about that, thought Dash grimly.

There was a beeping sound from the machine just then, and the hands were whisked back inside while the showerhead was activated and began to wash off the soapy suds. George's face emerged looking as daft and wide-eyed as before, his tongue still hanging out of his mouth.

'At least we might have solved the problem of his smelly breath,' muttered Dash. 'We must be grateful for small mercies.'

'That is unkind,' hissed Pippa, and she gave him another prod with her toe.

No one else had noticed this exchange as George was now being blow-dried. The bath had drained itself of the water and had turned itself into a super-speedy dryer by blowing hot air out of the plughole at the spaniel, rather like one of those wonderfully fast hand-dryers you sometimes find in posh public loos. The effect was as if George was in a wind tunnel! All his fur was

blown back and his ears were flapping madly, but the whole experience was over in a flash. His soft and silky fur was now perfectly dry, so the hands appeared again and a pair of clippers began to swiftly work away at the long hair on his body and the extra fur on his ears.

The minute the hands were finished, they disappeared, taking the clippers with them, and George was free to be picked up by Mrs Prim and given a well-deserved cuddle for surviving his ordeal. Not that he seemed to need it; he was still as calm as custard.

'Amazing!' cried Mrs Prim, smoothing her hands over her freshly groomed pooch. 'I have always been very happy with Mrs Fudge's service, as you know, Pippa,' she said. 'But I have to say, the effect this new machine has had on my Georgie is astounding. I could enter him for a show and he would win first prize, I am sure!' she trilled.

As she spoke, another pair of hands had emerged from the machine and was busily sweeping up the clippings from the spaniel's coat and disposing of them into a handy little bin in the side of the invention.

 164

'I'm glad you're pleased,' said Pippa. 'Isn't it wonderful to have such satisfied customers?' she added. And she gave Dash a look, which very clearly said: I told you so.

16

Pawology

A week later Raphael came into Chop 'n' Chat one afternoon to report that, 'Me frien' Bob – the postie in the village o' Much Snortin' – is askin' me about you, Mrs Fudge my darlin'! He say the villagers have heard you is the top-notch person to come to for hairdressin' and pooch pamperin'.'

'Much Snorting?' repeated Mrs Fudge. 'But that is over ten miles away. Surely the villagers have their own hair salon within walking distance.'

'Ah, but they is not havin' mir-ac-ul-ous machinery, is they, sweetness?' Raphael pointed out. 'No one who has heard o' the Foghorn treatments is goin' to settle for a borin' old wash and blow-dry now.' And he gave a little twirl on his rollerblades to show off his still sharp-looking haircut.

Raphael was right: results of the gossiping soon had the phone ringing so often that Pippa could have sworn it was overheating from the extra use.

'Now that Mrs Fudge needs to rest more, I haven't got time to answer the phone, let alone set the machines working, and make tea and cakes,' a flustered Pippa said to Tallulah after one particularly taxing afternoon.

'Well, we can fix the problem of answering the phone,' said Smug. 'All you need is an answering *machine*.'

'And what good would that be?' snapped Dash. 'Pippa will still have to call the people back, and that takes too much time as well!' He turned to Pippa and said, 'I'm sorry to say I told you so, but surely you can see that it is the machines that are the problem! They are making life more complicated rather than less.'

167

Tallulah coughed politely and said, 'May I suggest that we need to make a few contingency plans?'

'What?' said Pippa.

'We simply need to think ahead more,' put in Smug. 'The bookings should be better organized. For example, if you gave priority to the Crumblies, as a gesture to show how you appreciate their loyalty, then people from outside will have to understand that they cannot be slotted into the diary at the last minute.'

'But I can't turn *anyone* away!' exclaimed Pippa. 'Mrs Fudge has left *me* in charge this weekend. If I turn people away, she will get a bad name for herself and she will be upset with me.'

'Do not distress yourself,' said Smug. He rubbed his velvety-soft head against her legs. 'We can make a couple of simple adjustments here and there and you will find you can send twice as many clients through the machines as you have so far.'

Pippa immediately looked hopeful. 'Are you sure?'

But Dash was snarling gently. 'Pippa,' he said, 'have you not considered that speed is not always the answer? The reason this hair salon has been the success it has is that Mrs Fudge has lavished her time and energy on her clients. The very name of the salon, "Chop 'n' Chat", says it all. People have been coming here for company and conversation just as much as they have for hairdressing and dog grooming.'

'What are you saying, Dash?' Pippa asked irritably.

'Isn't it obvious?' said the miniature dachshund with a sigh. 'The machines do a marvellous job, granted. But that is *the only thing* they do. They don't listen to Millicent Beadle when she wants to talk about her aches and pains, do they? And they don't provide tea and sympathy when that poor harassed mother comes in with her naughty twin boys and needs more than five minutes' peace while you do their hair. Now she barely has time to sit down before the twins are done and dusted and out of here. Mrs Fudge used to provide so much more than a service. She was everyone's friend.'

'Oh, really,' put in Smug. 'I do think Dash is overreacting. Have any of your customers complained that Mrs Fudge is not chatting to them as much as she used to?' he asked.

Pippa shook her head firmly. 'No one has.'

'You see?' said Smug, smiling benignly at Dash. 'How about if we trial the idea of a faster setting while the girls are here to help? Then if Mrs Fudge feels up to it after her rest, she can sit and chat to people who are waiting – we could open up the garden as well and serve tea outside. It will lend the place a cafe atmosphere.'

Pippa thought this was an excellent idea. 'Yes!' she said, clapping her hands in delight. 'I like the sound of that.'

Smug turned and gave Dash a look that was part way between a sneer and a smile. 'We will take the

 170

machines home with us tonight then,' he said to Pippa. 'I am sure I can make the adjustments in no time.'

Foiled again, thought Dash. But not for much longer. I'll show this hound up for the nasty bit of work he really is. Why is that mind-reading machine in the Foghorns' place? And what was that coded note all about? What if they are spying for a rival hairdresser? Or what if they are spying for something much, much worse? He went cold as the thought took root in his mind. He swallowed hard. It's up to me, he decided. Pippa is not going to listen, so I must continue my detecting solo.

Poor Dash did not get very far however. He waited until the crazy duo had left Chop 'n' Chat and were well out of sight, and then he ran at top speed to their house, making sure he used bushes and shrubs as cover so that he would definitely not be spotted. But by the time he arrived at the Foghorns' residence, he found the cat flap securely fastened and the windows blacked out. He put his ear to the wall and heard all manner of peculiar noises from inside, which made the fact that he could not get in all the more frustrating.

'That surely proves they are up to no good!' he muttered. 'Why else would they make the place so secure?'

Dash had to wait a full twenty-four hours to find out what the Foghorns had been up to. He hardly slept a wink and paced up and down the kitchen so much that Mrs Fudge shut him out at one point, saying if he went on like that he would 'wear out the floor tiles'.

At last Tallulah and Smug arrived with the adjusted machines in tow.

'I have been giving some thought to what you said, Dash, about people coming with aches and pains and problems and so on,' Smug said. 'And I thought, why not add in a treatment which will

 172

completely distract the customer from their woes? Then they won't feel the need to talk about them.'

'Why not get rid of you for a start?' muttered Dash. 'That would get rid of my woes, I can tell you.'

'What's that?' Smug asked.

'Nothing,' said Pippa quickly, glaring at Dash. 'Tell us about your distraction idea.'

'Well, I've added a few relaxation options to the settings available,' said Smug, nodding to some new levers and cogs on the machines. 'Your customers can now have mini back massages and reflexology while they have their hair styled. And what's more, I've adapted things so that the machines can do more than one client at a time—'

'Er, what is Re Flox Elegy?' Pippa cut in.

'Re-flex-o-logy,' Tallulah corrected her. 'It's a kind of special foot massage – it can cure all sorts of aches and pains. It's miraculous.'

173

'Oh, Smug, you are clever!' cooed Pippa.

'No, he's not!' Dash yelped. 'Listen to me, these machines have a dangerous side to them. I'm telling you – I know all about it because . . .'

But no one was listening to him. It was as if his ability to communicate with humans had been turned off with the flick of one of Smug's infernal switches, he thought.

'Ah, but wait for the next bit,' Tallulah was saying, wiggling her eyebrows. 'I think you'll find Smug has surpassed himself this time. Not only has he invented relaxation treatments for the human clients, he has also created them FOR THEIR DOGS!' she finished. She swept her arm dramatically to gesture to Smug, who smiled primly and bowed.

'Yes,' he said. 'Paw massages or reflexology for dogs, if you will. Although I prefer to call it "pawology".'

Dash spluttered: 'Massages and paw rubs for *dogs*? Have you gone mad? Just because you like wearing

 174

spectacles and sitting up at table like a human, doesn't mean the rest of our species has gone raving bonkers like you.'

'Perhaps you would care to try the new functions before criticizing, Dash?' said Smug. He put his head on one side. 'I can assure you both the massage and the paw rub are a wonderful cure for stress. You will find that it simply flows out of you.'

'You are not getting me to sit in that machine,' Dash snapped.

'I think you'll find that you will feel decidedly less tetchy,' said Smug. He wrinkled his nose so that his spectacles rose and fell. Then he leaped forward and gave Dash a quick push towards the dog-grooming machine, flicking a switch with his nose as he did so.

'NO!' shouted Dash, wriggling and writhing. 'I've been here before. I know the mischief your inventions can wreak!' But he could not escape: he found himself held in place by the gloved

175

hands, and he looked up in horror at the familiar sink-plunger attachment, which lowered and clamped itself to his head.

'No!' he cried in alarm. 'Don't let that thing near me!' But then the hands, which were holding him on the chair, softened and began to push and prod his back very, very gently. Oh, if only I could have some peace and quiet away from these two, he wished. I just want to curl up in my basket and forget all this.

A clicking noise started up behind the machine the very moment that Dash had these thoughts, and a long sheet of paper fell on to the floor, displaying the words 'Just want to curl up in my basket and forget all this'.

But Dash did not see this as he was already feeling as though something had taken all the tension he had been holding right out of him. 'Ooooh,' he said as he began to relax. 'Actually, that's very . . . right a bit . . . aah, that's it . . . left a bit . . .'

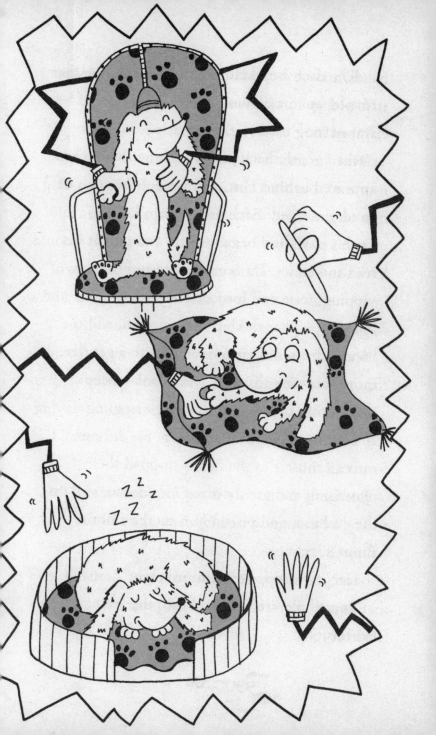

The dachshund closed his eyes and his lips turned up in a dreamy smile. Then, just as he was getting used to the sensation, he was pushed gently back into a cushion, which had appeared behind him, and yet another pair of hands emerged. Each took a firm hold of Dash's paws and began to rub and pull at his toes and claws. Dash gave a funny little yipping noise and his face creased up. 'Oh! No! Stop! That tickles!' he squealed, and the hands adjusted their movements to a gentler, more soothing rhythm. Dash took a deep shuddering breath and stopped wriggling. In fact, he was soon fast asleep. He did not move a muscle as the hands stopped their massaging and gently lifted him down, still on the cushion, and placed him on the floor at Pippa's feet.

Her jaw dropped in astonishment.

'Incredible, isn't it?' said the pug, seeing Pippa's expression.

'Amazing!' cried Pippa. She stooped to pick up the printout of Dash's thoughts. 'Smug, you are a genius. This machine can read our customers' minds.'

17

Da Da Daaaaaaaa! Disaster!

Within minutes of Smug's pawology demonstration, Penelope Smythe was at the door, looking breathless.

'I'm so sorry I'm late,' she said, as she plonked her shopping bags down on the salon floor. 'Sukie was giving me the runaround in the park! I didn't think I was going to be able to catch her. Oh my, I do feel rather stressed. Could I sit down for a moment?'

Tallulah wiggled her eyebrows at Pippa and said, 'Our first reflexology customer, wouldn't you say?'

'Stressed out and exhausted from chasing a doolally saluki,' said Smug, making a couple of discreet notes on his little pad. 'I think our machine will know exactly what to do.' He glanced quickly in Dash's direction, but the miniature dachshund was deeply asleep by now and was snoring contentedly.

Pippa followed Smug's gaze and laughed. 'If you can make Dash relaxed after the mood he's been in recently, I'm sure you can help Penelope.' Then turning to Penelope she said, 'We've got just the thing to make you feel better.' And she explained about the newly adapted machines.

'It does sound marvellous,' Penelope said. 'I could do with a massage.' She rolled her neck to show how stiff she was feeling.

'You will go all sleepy,' Pippa promised, showing her to the chair. 'It's lovely! You'll soon forget about the stressful morning you have had.'

Penelope had just got comfortable and was ready for the treatment to begin when the doorbell went again.

'Oh dear, I think our appointments schedule has got messed up,' said Pippa. She leafed quickly through the large black ledger where all the appointments were written. 'Great,' she sighed. 'Marble is due now. I expect even the machine's marvellous makeover has worn off already. It would be *her*, wouldn't it?'

'Never mind,' said Smug. He pushed his spectacles up his flat little nose. 'We can do them both at once, thanks to my adjustments. Tally and I will get Sukie ready while you go and answer the door to Marble.'

Pippa skedaddled down the hallway in answer to the ever more persistent ringing of the doorbell.

'About time too,' said Marble Wainwright, her potatoey face scrunched up into a sour sneer of disapproval. 'It's not very professional to keep your customers waiting, young lady.'

Pippa fixed a fake smile on to her face and said, 'Come in.'

If anyone could do with being sent to sleep by the new machine, it's Marble, she thought, as she led her into the salon. It would shut her up so I

 182

wouldn't have to listen to her moany old voice, for one thing.

'My, my,' said Marble sarcastically. 'We are going to town on the whole technology thing, aren't we?'

'Yes, we are,' Pippa snapped. And seeing as how you were so happy last time, I can't see that you have anything to complain about, she thought. But fixing the fake smile back on to her face she said, 'Please do take a seat next to Penelope, Marble.'

'Don't you want to know what style I want?' said the sour-faced lump.

Pippa nodded to Smug and said to Tallulah, 'I'll just get Snooks settled with Sukie. If you two — I mean, could you help make sure the two ladies are ready, Tally?'

'Certainly,' said Tallulah. And she flicked a switch.

The white-gloved hands shot out and began kneading Marble's knobbly old shoulders.

'Harrumph,' snorted Marble. 'Well, it's *quite* nice,

I suppose. I hope this thing is not going to massage my feet though,' she added crossly. 'I can't stand anyone touching my feet.'

Pippa eyed the grumpy woman's lumpy black shoes and thought, if Marble's feet are anything like as potatoey as her face, I don't think anyone would *want* to massage them.

But soon the machine was working its magic and Marble was smiling dreamily. 'I – oh, that's a bit better . . . Hmmm,' she said.

'Ahhh,' sighed Penelope, as she too began her treatment.

'Oooow!' Snooks whined, as he looked up in alarm at the sink plunger which was descending towards him.

'Rufff!' agreed Sukie, as the sink plunger seemed to sprout a twin which made its way to her silky head.

But even they were soon almost purring with pleasure as their pawology sessions began.

In fact, everyone in the room was so content that

that is quite probably why no one was prepared for what happened next.

WHOOSH! BELCH! BLEURGH!

There was an explosion of the most worrying noises, followed by an eruption of paper which shot out of the machines, hitting the ceiling like fireworks and falling in a cascade so that everyone could plainly read the words which streamed over the surface of the printout.

'Oh no!' cried Pippa, as she realized what the words said. 'Can't you stop it?'

But it was too late! Penelope's thoughts were there in large type for everyone to read:

THAT MARBLE WAINWRIGHT IS THE
RUDEST PERSON I HAVE EVER
MET. JUST MY LUCK TO BE SAT
NEXT TO *HER*. *AND* SHE SMELLS
OF ONIONS. SHE COULD DO WITH
A GOOD WASHING-DOWN!

'WHAT? How dare you –!' shrieked Marble, as she read the words falling in front of her eyes.

'Smug?' said Tallulah, a note of panic rising in her voice. 'I think something's gone wrong.'

'Dash! Dash!' cried Pippa, shaking the little dachshund. 'I need your help.'

But Dash could not be woken.

'What have you done to him?' Pippa shouted at Smug. She was beginning to see that her poochy friend must have been right about the machines all along. 'Oh, Dash,' she said. 'I'm sorry! I should have listened to you!'

'Don't panic,' the pug yelped, running round and round the machines, flicking switches and pulling levers. 'Don't panic!'

'Why don't you take your own advice and stop and think about what you're doing?!' Pippa yelled.

Next, to add to the confusion, Sukie and Snooks had started up an alarming racket too. Pippa rushed to their sides just as more paper was catapulted out

186

of the printer. The thoughts of Sukie and Snooks, and unfortunately Marble too, were now pouring out in huge letters, there for all to see:

THIS IS THAT SMUG PUG'S FAULT! SOMEBODY GET HIM!

I'VE HAD ENOUGH OF BEING MARBLE'S DOG. I WISH THAT MACHINE WOULD WASH HER AWAY!

I HAVE ALWAYS DETESTED THAT PENELOPE SMYTHE WITH HER STUCK-UP ATTITUDE. I WOULD LIKE TO SEE THAT SMILE WIPED OFF HER FACE!

'Well!' cried Penelope indignantly. 'That's ripe, coming from you!'

'Let me at her!' growled Marble, struggling to reach Penelope.

'SMUG, DO SOMETHING!' yelled Pippa at the top of her lungs.

And then lots of things happened at once.

Smug was grabbed by yet more mechanical hands, which had appeared seemingly from nowhere, and was thrown right out of the window; Penelope's head was held in a vice-like grip while the hands which had been massaging her began rubbing vigorously at her face (to wipe the smile off presumably) and Marble was lashed to her seat with a long length of rope and an entire bottle of shampoo was dumped on to her head in one go!

Pippa felt her chest tighten as she watched.

'What's *happening*?' she cried above the screaming and the shouting and the clanking of machinery. She knew she should do something, but she could not think what. Her brain had frozen and her legs

and arms had turned to lead. She was rooted to the spot.

Where was Tallulah? Pippa whirled around to find her friend among the chaos, but all she could see was whirring machinery and frenzied customers shrieking and wailing as they were pummelled and pushed and thumped around by the monstrous inventions.

Then, just as suddenly as the commotion had started, it all stopped. The white-gloved hands dropped limply to the sides of the machines, the flashing lights were extinguished and the horrible noises ceased. Pippa could hear her heart banging against her ribs. Marble and Penelope had both fainted and the dogs were simply whimpering softly, cowering in their places on the dog-grooming machine. The eerie calm was suddenly broken by a loud yawn from somewhere near Pippa's feet.

'Yaaaaawwwn! Ah, that's better,' said a familiar voice. 'I must say, one does feel so much better after a good kip.'

189

'Dash?' whispered Pippa, crouching down to her old friend. She held out her arms and the little dog jumped into them.

'Hello!' he said cheerily. Then, 'Oh. My. Goodness!' he yelped, as he took in the scene of devastation. 'What on earth has gone on here?'

'That's just what I was going to ask,' said another familiar voice. It was Mrs Fudge, who had been woken up from *her* nap by all the fuss.

'Oh, Mrs Fudge . . . Dash . . . I'm sorry! I'm sorry! I'm sorry!' wailed poor Pippa. She put her face in her hands and wept. 'I should have listened to you. I should never have used these machines—'

'You're telling me, young lady!' said a deep, gravelly voice.

At that, everyone spun around. Standing in the door behind Mrs Fudge was a very tall, spindly old man with a round red-bearded face which was crowned with crazy, bouncy, fluffy red hair, in which were nestled several pairs of black-framed spectacles. The man was wearing a white coat of the sort hospital doctors have, except that his was covered in pockets, which were stuffed full of notebooks, pens, pencils and rulers. Pippa realized she knew exactly who he was.

'Wh-who are you?' stammered Mrs Fudge.

'I am Professor Foghorn,' said the man. 'But

more to the point, who are you? And what *have* you done with my Mesmerizing Mind Machine? It's barely recognizable in that state. And I suppose you have made off with my Bubble-Car-Scooter-Mobile as well!'

18

The Mesmerizing Mind Machine

Before anyone could ask exactly what the professor meant by his Mesmerizing Mind Machine or indeed his Bubble-Car-Scooter-Mobile, there was a small noise from one of the inventions.

It was Penelope, who seemed to have come out of her faint. 'Excuse me,' she said quietly, 'do you think you could let me and Sukie out of these – things?'

'Things?' barked the professor. 'THINGS? Madam, I'll have you know that my Mesmerizing Mind Machine is an extremely important and, until today, top-secret design. I have been in touch with the highest echelons of the world's governments in developing this idea. In fact, only this morning

I was in Russia at the World Convention of Mastermind Geniuses, explaining the concept of Mind-Reading and Its Use in International Spy Rings: I left Tally a note to say I'd gone – in code of course.' He paused and scratched his head as if he had forgotten what it was he was talking about.

'You see!' Dash hissed. 'I TOLD YOU!'

'Told me what?' Pippa hissed back. 'I can't understand a word he's talking about!'

The professor's expression had cleared. 'Ah yes!' he shouted, making everyone jump. 'I came home to do a final trial on my inventions before selling them, only to find they had been dismantled in my absence and my Bubble-Car-Scooter-Mobile had also GONE! There has been some unspeakable thievery going on around here, unless I am much mistaken,' he finished.

'I – I'm not sure I understand all the words you've just said,' simpered Penelope, 'but you do seem very cross. Perhaps if you were to get me out of this, er, invention, I could help?'

Marble Wainwright had chosen that moment to come round too. 'Help? You? You couldn't help a person put their pants on—'

'Excuse *me*!' protested Penelope.

'Oh, for goodness sake,' said the professor crossly. 'How can a person have an intelligent conversation around here with all this wittering going on?' He crossed the room in two long strides and flicked a switch on the machine, which immediately sent Penelope and Marble to sleep!

Pippa had been about to protest at the machine being switched on again, but could not help sniggering at the way the professor had swiftly silenced Marble Wainwright.

Now that's the sort of invention we could definitely do with at Chop 'n' Chat, she thought.

The professor whirled back to face Mrs Fudge, Dash and Pippa. 'So,' he continued, 'are you going to tell me how you came to steal my

inventions and mess around with them in such an insolent fashion?'

'Grandfather, you shouldn't be cross with Pippa and Mrs Fudge, you know.'

'Tallulah?' Pippa breathed, turning to see her friend lurking in the hallway.

Tallulah was looking very shamefaced indeed,

and Smug seemed to be pretending he did not have the faintest idea what was going on. He was wearing his pink helmet though, which the professor immediately snatched from him.

'I will explain everything,' said Tallulah, 'but first can we all sit down and have a cup of tea? And I know Grandfather would love one of your scones, Mrs Fudge,' she pleaded.

'Scones?' said the professor. He dropped the helmet absent-mindedly and pulled down a pair of spectacles to peer around the room as if he hoped the scones might be hiding somewhere nearby. 'Scones, you say? Now you're talking.' He seemed to have forgotten how angry he had been.

'Er, quite,' said Mrs Fudge. 'But what about poor Marble and Penelope?'

'They'll be all right for now,' Pippa said hastily. 'Tea and scones?'

'Yes, yes,' said the professor. He rubbed his tummy and licked his lips. Then he reached out and

197

picked up a tub of hair wax and opened his mouth wide as if to take a bite.

'Grandfather!' Tallulah whisked the pot away. 'That's not a scone! You're wearing the wrong glasses,' she pointed out. 'Those are your reading ones.' And she reached up to pull the correct pair of spectacles out of the professor's bird's nest of hair.

'Quite so, quite so,' said the professor, blinking quickly. 'Onwards to the tea and scones then!'

Once everyone had been seated and given refreshments, Tallulah said she would explain.

'I need to apologize to you all,' she said. She took a deep breath. 'Including Grandfather.'

'What's that?' said the professor, through a mouthful of crumbs.

Smug rolled his eyes. 'Go on, Tally,' he said.

'It is true that Grandfather had been working on a secret mind-reading invention,' Tallulah began, looking at Pippa and Mrs Fudge. 'And Smug and

 198

I thought we could borrow bits of it while he was away. We were going to bring all the parts back. We just wanted to try out the idea of reading customers' minds to give them exactly what they wanted. It was wrong of us, we know that now,' she finished quietly.

'But that was so *dangerous*!' Dash protested. 'To take parts of one machine and mix them with another – it doesn't take a genius to work that out. And I thought *you* were a genius,' he added, sneering at Smug. 'In any case, we were perfectly all right before you came along, thank you. All you have done is make matters worse for Mrs Fudge, not better.'

The professor had paused in his munching and was staring at Dash, his mouth wide open, a scone midway to his lips. 'Excuse me,' he said eventually. 'Have I got the wrong glasses on again? I thought I just heard that dachshund speak!'

'You did,' Pippa and Tallulah chorused.

There was a long and awkward silence as the

professor peered at the two girls through one set of spectacles after the other, while Tallulah's face went redder and redder and Pippa began to shuffle in her chair.

'Are – are you all right, Professor dear?' asked Mrs Fudge.

Tallulah's grandfather slapped the table, making everyone jump, and shouted, 'Fascinating!' He let out a roar of laughter. 'So you too are conversant with the canine,' he said, now staring at Pippa and Mrs Fudge in turn.

'Eh?' said Pippa. This being-at-a-loss-for-words business was becoming quite a habit where Tallulah's family were concerned.

'He means that you can understand the dogs,' said Smug.

'I knew that,' muttered Pippa.

'I didn't, dear,' admitted Mrs Fudge.

'But this is *marvellous*,' the professor went on. 'I thought Smug was a one-off. Or rather, that the reason Tallulah and I understood him was due to

our highly developed intellects. Most interesting.'
He paused. 'But this must mean that you, madam,
and your – granddaughter, is it? You must be as
erudite as we are.'

'No,' Pippa snapped. 'I'm not her granddaughter.
And you might be a rude whatever-you-said, but I
am *not*, thank you very much—'

'Erudite. It means you must both be really
clever,' Smug translated again. 'Although,
personally, I think that's a little generous of the
professor.'

'Er, if I may continue,' said the professor. 'I
am extremely impressed with you, Mrs Toffee,' he
said.

'Mrs Fudge, actually,' said Pippa.

'Yes, yes,' Professor Foghorn sighed impatiently.
'Your powers of interpretation of the canine mind
are proof enough that you can handle one of my
inventions. So, I have an idea.'

'Good grief,' Dash muttered. 'Do you think you
can explain it in plain English?'

201

'Of course,' said the professor. 'You are in need of extra help around the place, which is why my granddaughter and Smug thought they should assist you.'

'Erm, yes,' said Mrs Fudge, who felt shy after being called 'really clever' by a professor.

'And I am in need of some way of showcasing my Mesmerizing Mind Machine. If I am to sell my idea, I need to prove that it will work . . .' He paused and looked thoughtful again. '*And* my granddaughter is in need of a friend and a place to go after school and at the weekends when I am busy with my projects . . .'

Mrs Fudge looked anxious. 'What are you thinking? Only, it seems to me, without wanting to be rude, your machines have got us into a spot of bother here today.'

'Clearly that is because I was not here to supervise,' retorted the professor. 'If Tally and Smug had only consulted me first, I could have ensured that no disasters occurred.' He tutted.

'Follow me. I shall put things right immediately.'

And he strode back into the salon with everyone hot on his heels. He made straight for the machines and circled them, talking to himself and flicking switches and levers, making tiny adjustments to the position of dials and plugging and unplugging various attachments.

'There, that should do it for now,' he said. And with one final press of a button, he stood back and watched.

Pippa squeezed her eyes tight shut. 'I can't bear to see what happens next,' she whispered, as she feared yet another catastrophe was about to occur.

But there were no loud noises, no explosions. Nothing alarming happened at all, other than a very loud yawning sound from Marble and some sleepy little squeaks from Penelope and the dogs.

'Oh my! What a lovely, relaxing pampering session,' said Penelope, stretching out her arms.

'Yes, I do believe that's the most wonderful

experience I've ever had,' said Marble. 'These inventions of yours seem to get better and better, Mrs Fudge,' she added politely. 'I do hope the machines are staying here for good.'

'Good heavens,' muttered Dash. 'Has your machine given Marble a brain transplant, Professor?'

'Oh, can't you say something complimentary for once?' growled Smug.

'Not if it means you are staying here for good as well,' snarled Dash.

Mrs Fudge patted his head. 'Now, now,' she said. 'I think it's about time that these little pooches put their differences behind them and agreed to disagree, don't you?'

'Oh, Mrs F.!' protested Pippa. 'Don't you start talking like a Foghorn! What do you mean?'

'I mean,' said Mrs Fudge, 'that it would be nice if we could ALL be friends.'

'It most certainly would, dear madam,' said the professor, taking Mrs Fudge's hand and kissing it.

Tallulah and Pippa exchanged a look of triumph.

'Here's to happy endings!' said Pippa, bending down to give Dash a hug.

'If you say so,' Dash said with a sigh. 'But just remember,' he said to Smug, '*I* am still top dog around here.'

The Bit at the End
Where We Say Goodbye

Well, look at that! We have come to the end – and, as Pippa said, a very happy end it was too. The professor stayed in Crumbly-under-Edge and was true to his word about looking after his machines, so there were no more accidents at Chop 'n' Chat.

I should think not.
I am a professor,
after all.

Tallulah and Pippa stayed friends forever.

We did!

And all the Crumblies stayed loyal to Mrs Fudge
forever too. Best of all, even Smug and Dash learned
to get along and be friendly.

If you can't
beat 'em, join
'em.

I think you mean two heads are better than one.

And they made a promise to Muffles to lead a quieter life and not disturb her snoozes so often.

Miaoooow!

In fact, everything turned out so well for the
pooch-pampering parlour that you could say
everyone felt rather, well, *smug* about it!

speak for yourself!

Thank you, I was.

This story was written by a lady called **Anna Wilson**. She lives in a town which is rather like Crumbly-under-Edge, where there is a hair salon a bit like Mrs Fudge's: the ladies there are just as lovely as Mrs Fudge (although not as old) and they love to eat cake. **Anna** has two cats, Jet and Inky, who are quite like Muffles (except they are black), and a pooch called Kenna (who doesn't actually like being pampered, unless it involves food). She also has three chickens who lay eggs that are perfect for cake-baking. Titch, one of the chickens, quite likes being pampered. **Anna** is thinking of setting up a Poultry-Pampering Parlour just for her.

If you would like to find out more about **Anna** and her books you can visit www.annawilson.co.uk. Or you can write to her:

Anna Wilson
c/o Macmillan Children's Books
20 New Wharf Road
London
N1 9RR

Anna would love to see your pet photos too! But don't forget to enclose a stamped addressed envelope if you want her to return them to you.

Monkey Business

Anna Wilson

It's so BORING having normal pets!

For Felix and Flo, animals are the NUMBER ONE
TOP PRIORITY in life. And although Felix loves
his pets (a lazy dog, an angry cat and a noisy hamster),
what he really wants is to look after an animal which
is EXOTIC and DIFFERENT. Will Flo's brilliant
and FOOLPROOF plan get Felix his perfect pet –
or will it just send him bananas?

A side-splittingly chaotic story about schemes,
dreams and monkeying around.

The Poodle Problem

Anna Wilson

Welcome to the Pooch Parlour,
where mystery-solving has become
this season's hottest new look!

Something very strange is going on in the cosy
town of Crumbly-under-Edge! Join Pooch Parlour
regulars Dash the dachshund and his human
friend Pippa 'chat-till-the-cows-come-home'
Peppercorn as they uncover a dastardly plot
involving oodles of snooty poodles . . .

The first in the bonkers Pooch Parlour series

The Dotty Dalmatian

Anna Wilson

Welcome to the Pooch Parlour,
where pets get pampered
and mysteries get solved!

Mrs Fudge has hired a cool new assistant who
is an instant favourite with all the dogs. Pippa
Peppercorn isn't so sure – there's something
strange about the new girl. Meanwhile a mysterious
spotty dog is causing havoc around town . . . Will
Pippa and Dash the talking dachshund save the day?

The second in the magical Pooch Parlour series